ALOHA LOVE

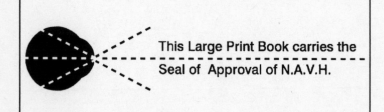

This Large Print Book carries the
Seal of Approval of N.A.V.H.

ALOHA LOVE

YVONNE LEHMAN

THORNDIKE PRESS
A part of Gale, Cengage Learning

GALE
CENGAGE Learning®

Detroit • New York • San Francisco • New Haven, Conn • Waterville, Maine • London

GALE
CENGAGE Learning·

LIBRARY OF CONGRESS CATALOGING-IN-PUBLICATION DATA

Lehman, Yvonne.
    Aloha love / by Yvonne Lehman. — Large print ed.
       p. cm. — (Thorndike Press large print Christian fiction)
    "Aloha Brides; bk 1."
    ISBN-13: 978-1-4104-4437-0 (hardcover)
    ISBN-10: 1-4104-4437-6 (hardcover)
    1. Young women—Fiction. 2. Widowers—Fiction. 3. Horse farms—Fiction. 4. Hawaii—Social life and customs—19th century—Fiction. I. Title.
PS3562.E43A79 2012
813'.54—dc23   2011045444

Published in 2012 by arrangement with Barbour Publishing, Inc.

Printed in Mexico
1 2 3 4 5 6 7 16 15 14 13 12

Dear Readers,

When I consented to write three historical Hawaii novels, I had no idea there was so much exciting, interesting history. When developing fictional characters, I need to be true to history, such as the first Hawaiian to become a Christian, working around tsunamis and volcanic eruptions, first missionaries, royalty, paniolas (cowboys), annexation, picture-bride era, and World War II. I sincerely hope these stories will be as intriguing to you as they were for me to write. I appreciate the loyalty of my readers through the years and look forward to hearing from you and any new readers. My desire is that you see how God worked in the Hawaiian Islands and know that He is always ready to work in the lives of we who believe. My hope is that you will be thoroughly entertained by my stories.

I wish God's richest blessings upon you.

Yvonne

To Carmen Leal, my writer-friend who lives in Hawaii and made *paniolo* suggestions that inspired my plot ideas for *Aloha Love* and gave me the idea for its sequel, *Picture Bride.*

CHAPTER 1

1889, The Big Island, Hawaii

"The Little People won't let the Night Marchers hurt me, will they, Daddy?" five-year-old Leia asked as Makana Lalama MacCauley tucked her in for the night.

"You know they'll keep you safe, Leia. And so will I."

Her little pink lips turned into a smile, and her big brown eyes — so like her mother's — held confidence that her daddy would not tell her a lie. *"Aloha au la oe,* Daddy."

Mak bent to kiss her forehead. "I love you, too."

Tucking his daughter in safely for the night was a special time, but he dreaded what would follow. As her eyes closed, his smiled faded. Her words resounded in his mind, but there were places in his heart even they couldn't touch. Reaching over to turn down the wick in the whale-oil lamp was like inviting the chill, beckoning the darkness with its never-ending feeling of loss, that aching loneliness, the unfairness of it all.

When Mak left the room, leaving the door open a few inches, his mother stepped from the doorway of her room. Observing the expression of displeasure on his mother's face, he braced himself for a reprimand. They walked down the hallway and into the kitchen.

He didn't sit, and she didn't follow her usual routine of brewing a cup of hot tea. Instead, she sighed and held onto the back of a chair. "I heard what Leia said, Mak. How long are you going to let her believe in those idols and myths?"

"She's a child, Mother. And the myths of the Little People are fun. The paniolos' children she plays with tell these stories like my friends and I did when I was a child. Besides," he added, "I believed in faeries, brownies, and silkies."

"But you were taught by your dad and me the difference between myth and truth."

"Don't you teach her the truth, Mother?"

"She needs to know what her dad believes, too."

His stare caused her to look away. They both knew his current beliefs were not fit for a child's ears.

He shook his head and walked toward the screen door rather than say something disrespectful to his mother.

But his mother did not allow him the same courtesy. She constantly badgered him about God and letting Leia go to the mission school. His own early education had been at the mission school, so he knew his mother was teaching Leia more than she would learn there — and in less time.

They'd been through this many times. With a deep sigh, he walked out into the calm night. His heart was heavy. How could he keep his little girl safe when he hadn't kept his own wife safe? And how could he give Leia assurance that God would keep her safe when he had stopped believing in the love of the God who had let his young wife die? He and Leia needed Maylea so much.

His mother kept raising the question, "Is your own child never to learn to ride, Mak?"

How could he force his daughter on a horse when her mother had been killed by one? He, who trained horses and bred them for the royal races, would not insist his daughter learn to ride. He had not been able to calm her fear, or his for her, and horses sensed that. But his mother was right, Leia was almost six years old.

Leia had become as adamant about what she wanted as his mother, and it seemed they both were taking sides against him.

He lifted his eyes to the sky, star-spangled with lights of blinking mockery, a sharp contrast to his mind, punctuated with his mother's questions, his daughter's resoluteness, and his own indecision. He bent his head and gazed at the dusty path leading to the carriage-house stables.

This was a lonely time of night. The moonlight wasn't as pleasant as it used to be. The stars not as bright. The quiet was not comforting. His cattle were in the fields; his horses grazing or in the larger stables. His paniolos would have gone home or settled in the bunkhouse.

Strange how a man's life and confidence could take a 180-degree turn in so short a time. He'd thought himself a man after marrying Maylea and taking over the care of the ranch and his mother when his dad died. God was in His heaven, and all was right with the world. But all was not right with this world. His mother was now taking care of him. She and his daughter seemed to question his every move.

He would consider their requests after the

race. Leia was young. There was plenty of time.

This was not the time to make such decisions. Next year, he'd be a different man. There was the upcoming race. He must attend to that. He walked into the stable and breathed in the aroma of rich earth, straw, and horseflesh so welcome to his sense of hope.

Hope?

No. More than hope.

Not seeing his jockey, Chico, he assumed the man had retired to his room in the carriage-house part of the building.

Mak strolled over to the great racehorse that only he had trained — that only he and his jockey had ridden. Panai was the most beautiful horse he'd ever seen — midnight black with a streak of white down his face from his ears to his nose. He had the eyes of a winner, one with the desire to just be given the chance. He was almost ready.

Panai would bring Mak the victory he must have, his number one goal: to win.

Then, and only then, could Mak find relief from his grief and anger.

Mother and son . . . racing for the coveted Big Island Cup.

Ill-conceived it might be, but Mak would have his revenge.

CHAPTER 2

April 1889, Texas

Jane looked out on the range from her upstairs window and saw the cows wandering aimlessly, likely chewing their cud, their only concern swishing away flies with their tails.

What a life.

But would hers be any more exciting?

Realizing she was twisting the impressive diamond on her finger that she'd worn for more than a year, she stopped, studied it, and understood anew what it represented.

Jane Marie Buckley and Austin Price were made for each other. They grew up believing it because their parents told them so. Having heard it repeatedly through the years was probably like cud chewing. She'd had to swallow it. But lately, the thought of being a married woman was hard to stomach.

Realizing she was once again moving the

diamond ring up to her knuckle and back again, she stopped. It seemed that right hand of hers was always trying to take the ring off her left.

She had nothing against Austin. No one seemed to know of any fellow more suitable for her. And nothing was really wrong with him. She liked him. Furthermore, she loved him.

The Buckleys were in cattle and horses. The Prices were in oil. Her daddy would throw her the most fantastic wedding Texas had ever seen — that is, if she ever set a date. Things kept coming up. There'd been her daddy's cattle drives and Austin's college education, Matilda's embarking on another excursion, Jane's going off to college — or not wanting her wedding to be at the same time as a friend's.

The wedding part delighted her, but she wasn't too keen on marriage. She'd seen too many friends marry and become dull and boring when they weren't frazzled over what to do with their children.

The men fared well, but the women — that was another matter. Yet what else was there for an educated, marriageable young woman?

As a privileged married woman, at least she wouldn't have to worry about the flies.

While strolling over the green lawns avoiding the cow patties, her swishing fan would flick the flies away. Another thought made her giggle. Would a fly dare to land on the likes of Mrs. Jane Marie Buckley Price?

The fast clip of horses' hooves and the clanking of turning wheels on the cobblestone drive broke her reverie. Leaning closer to the window, she saw the fancy coach come into view. That could be none other than Aunt Matilda Russell Buckley — her most exciting relative in the world. With a tinge of sadness, Jane remembered the shocking explosion at an oil refinery several years before that had killed her dad's only brother and had left Aunt Matilda a widow.

Come to think of it, Matilda fared quite well as a single woman. But again, the word *widow* had a more respectable ring to it than *spinster.* Jane cringed at the thought of being married just yet, but she certainly didn't want to be a spinster.

Did she?

She would prefer to be a widow like Matilda. Not that she wanted Austin dead. She just wanted to have an exciting life like Matilda. Seeing her aunt emerge from the carriage, Jane was reminded anew that her aunt was nothing less than colorful in her long green skirt with a matching traveling vest over a white blouse with flowing sleeves. She'd been told by a few friends and acquaintances that she and Matilda were a lot alike, but Jane felt like a washed-out version of Matilda. Her own hair was brown, her eyes blue green, and her skin less glowing. She pinched her cheeks but knew it to be a futile gesture to appear more attractive. Matilda would be stunning.

"Matilda," Jane called from the window. Her aunt looked up, revealing her beautiful peaches-and-cream skin, reddened lips, and copper-colored hair beneath a wide green hat adorned with graceful plumes. Matilda waved vigorously, and her lips spread into a delighted smile. Even from that distance, Jane could see her aunt's green eyes.

Turning from the window, Jane dashed down the hall and sped down the wide, curved staircase to the foyer. Inez had apparently heard the coach and was hanging her white apron on a peg in a closet below the staircase. The meticulous Inez closed the door, then smoothed her black dress and lifted her hand to make sure her black hair was not in disarray before opening the door to a visitor.

"I'll get it," Jane said. "It's Matilda." A dreaded look appeared in Inez's eyes. Nevertheless, she reopened the closet door

17

to take out her apron and return to her duties.

After all, it was only Matilda, whom Inez considered "that worldly woman."

Pilar, the seventeen-year-old daughter of Inez, held a different opinion. The girl yelled from the kitchen, "Did you say Matilda?"

Jane nodded.

Inez warned, "Remember your place, Pilar."

But Pilar's "Ohhh" sounded like she thought royalty had arrived.

Jane shared that thought as she swung open the front door and hurried toward her aunt. Feeling quite plain in a simple cream-colored day dress, Jane nevertheless fell into her aunt's arms for a warm, meaningful embrace while they expressed their joy at being together after a three-month absence.

"Ahem."

The cough from the coachman brought to their attention that Matilda's bags had been deposited on the wide, front porch of Buckley House. Matilda reached into the front of her blouse and withdrew a small purse from which she took a gold coin that widened the eyes of the driver.

"Thank you, ma'am," he crowed exuberantly, bobbing his head of collar-length hair. "Been a pleasure, ma'am."

By that time, Inez stood in front of the open door while Pilar came out to help with the bags.

"Oh, if I'd known" — Pilar's eyes widened, and her chest rose with her rapid breathing — "I would have put flowers in your room, and —"

Matilda waved her graceful hand. Sparkling rings adorned several fingers. "Oh, I'm sure your mother will excuse you long enough to pick some flowers from the garden."

"Yes, ma'am. I know she will."

Inez smiled stiffly, but they all knew if Matilda requested something, it would be done. Pilar rushed to take hold of the largest bag and tug it inside. Matilda was not opposed to picking up her own bags, but allowing Pilar to do it meant a generous tip from Matilda, perhaps a gold coin or two.

Jane stopped at the bottom of the staircase when Matilda did. "I assume suppertime is as usual," her aunt said.

"Of course." Jane laughed. "Nothing ever changes around here except a new bull, the birthing of a few more cows, and Austin's bringing in another oil well."

Matilda lifted her graceful hand in a dismissive gesture and looked toward the great chandelier hanging from the two-story-high ceiling. Then she focused on Jane with widened eyes and a serious tone. "I will fill you in at suppertime."

Matilda grabbed Jane's shoulders and stared into her eyes. With a flourish, she turned, lifted her skirts, and ascended the stairs.

Jane had no way of knowing what Matilda had on her mind. But one thing was certain. Aunt Matilda's appearance meant something momentous had occurred or was about to.

And it could only be disastrous . . . or sensational.

CHAPTER 3

"Buck, I bear news from the paradise in the Pacific," Aunt Matilda said after she greeted Jane's father with an exuberant embrace.

"After grace, we'll look forward to hearing it." John Buckley stepped back from Matilda and smoothed his mustache as if it had been disturbed, although not even the top of Matilda's elaborate coiffure had touched it. He stepped over and pulled out a chair for her from the dining room table.

Jane could hardly wait for his prayer to end. The Hawaiian stories she had heard about for many years were better than any fairy tale. She figured Matilda exaggerated, but she didn't mind.

"It's Pansy," Matilda said as soon as she and Jane said *Amen* after Jane's father asked the Lord's blessing on the sumptuous meal. Pilar would get another gold piece out of this dinner of the choicest beef, mid-April spinach from the garden, canned vegetables from last year's harvest, and the best corn bread that ever came out of an oven. Inez was too proud to accept money other than her wages.

"Pilar, you may remember Pansy," Matilda said, addressing the young woman who stood with her hands folded in front of her white apron as she waited to see if anyone needed anything. Much to the chagrin of Jane's father, Matilda never excluded anyone from her conversations and had point-blank said that anyone who didn't like it was downright snooty. So Mr. Buckley took it on the chin when Matilda gave a thumb gesture for Pilar to have a seat at the table.

Matilda continued her elucidation. Of course Jane and her father knew exactly who Pansy was. Pilar probably did, too, but Matilda had her way of doing things. She looked at Pilar and explained, "Pansy Russell is my brother's wife. Kermit Russell is a pastor in Hawaii. He never liked the name Kermit. Pansy wrote a long time ago that everybody in Hawaii calls him Pastor, Brother, or Reverend Russell, so she started calling him Russ. I need to remember that."

Pilar nodded. Matilda lifted a forkful of mashed potatoes in which Pilar would have included scads of fresh butter, milk, and mayonnaise. It appeared to melt in Matilda's mouth; then she washed it down with sweet tea. "This is an aside," she said, "but I simply must compliment Pilar." She faced the young cook again. "You milked the cow, churned the cream, and made this butter, did you not?"

"Yes ma'am."

"Oh, at a time like this I am so grateful for you." She took another sip of tea. "Now, for my news."

They all waited. Although her dad had cut his meat and popped it into his mouth, Jane hadn't taken a bite of anything.

"Pansy is ill." Matilda took another sip of tea as if needing some libation to relieve her dry mouth so she could get through the announcement.

A sympathetic "Ohhh" sounded from Pilar.

Jane glanced at her father, who simply alternated focus between Matilda and his food. They were accustomed to her drama. But this sounded serious.

Matilda reached into the pocket of her skirt and drew out a sheet of light blue paper. "This is exactly what Pansy wrote." She unfolded the paper and read:

My doctors do not expect me to live. I'm ready to go if the Lord doesn't see fit to heal me. I want to be buried on the Big

Island that has become home to me. My only regret is that I might have to leave my husband and dear children and friends in Hawaii.

Pilar's eyes popped. "She has children?"

"School children, dear." Matilda reached over and patted Pilar's folded hands. She stopped talking, as if one act of a stage play had ended and she was getting ready to begin the next. "I'm totally parched from that long carriage ride." She took another sip of tea.

"But this," Matilda said, closing her eyes and shaking her head. "This is what just about sends me over the edge."

Hearing Matilda's heavy sigh, Jane watched her dad respectfully lower his fork to his plate. Jane folded her hands on her lap. Pilar held her hands over her mouth and nose. Anything that could send Matilda over the edge would be colossal.

She took a deep breath and then read each word with great deliberation:

Russ needs you, Matilda. He will need you more after I'm gone. You know you're like a sister to me. If at all possible, I want to see you. But I don't know if I can live that long.

Jane watched Matilda swallow hard. She cleared her throat and continued to read:

One of our dear church members, Makana MacCauley, has taken over some of my classes. I wrote to you about the MacCauley tragedy. He has his own problems, so I don't know how long this will last. If at all possible, please come.

Knowing that Matilda could burst into tears, bellow out an unseemly string of unacceptable syllables, become uncannily silent, or even throw things, they waited.

Mr. Buckley ventured to mumble, "I'm sorry."

Matilda sat with her finger bent against her lips and her eyes lowered. After a long moment, she laid her hand in her lap and nodded. "I thought Pansy had mentioned a Rose MacCauley before. I remembered because she has the name of a flower. Seems there was some family tragedy. Something about her son's wife being in a terrible accident." Her head moved from side to side, and she sighed. "Perhaps I could be of some help to her." She smiled. "We who have suffered loss have a responsibility to comfort others."

She let that sink in. Jane found it amazing

that her aunt could say so much without really saying it and leave no room for debate. Matilda had lost her husband. Jane's dad had lost his wife and brother. Jane had lost her mother and uncle.

Her daddy must be thinking they all had a responsibility to others. And she was sure the Bible said so.

Matilda held out her glass to Pilar. "Could you freshen my tea, dear?"

"Oh, of course." Pilar stood and pushed her chair back under the table. She went to the sideboard, dumped the tea into the sink, filled the glass with ice from the icebox, and poured the tea from a crystal pitcher.

"I must go," Matilda said dramatically after the tea was set at her plate and Pilar had moved away to await any further directive.

"Yes, I understand your concern," Mr. Buckley said. "How long since you've seen Pansy?"

"Ten years," Matilda said. "I've been remiss, but of course when your dear brother was alive, I traveled wherever he suggested."

Jane knew her dad would be skeptical about that. Matilda rarely did anything she didn't want to do.

She looked at them again. "I must go to

Hawaii. Perhaps Pansy will still be alive by the time I arrive. If not, I need to comfort my brother. Maybe I could help out in that school. As you know, Kermit — I mean Russell — Russell is my only living blood relative."

Jane knew her dad would be thinking that when Jane's mother had died, Matilda had been right there to help in any way. She'd become not a mother, but a wonderful friend and companion to Jane and a big help to Jane's dad. When her husband had died, Matilda had been able to comfort Jane's dad with tales of the wonderful life his brother had lived.

"I understand." Jane saw compassion in her dad's eyes as he looked at Matilda. "When are you leaving?"

Matilda lifted her napkin from her lap to her nose for a moment and sniffed lightly. Her voice trembled. "How can I, Buck? A lady of my position cannot travel that far alone. I must have a companion."

Jane's heart almost leapt from her chest. The glance between her and Matilda before her aunt again slid her gaze to John Buckley spoke volumes. They both knew who that companion must be.

Jane's dad nodded. "What about your friend who traveled to California with you?

Would she not accompany you?"

"Oh no, Buck. She fears water. Would barely put her toe in the Pacific Ocean. She would never step foot on a ship that would keep her on the water for months."

"You might advertise," he said.

"There isn't time." She folded the blue paper, and her lower lip trembled. "And how could I trust a stranger?" She returned the note to her skirt pocket. "I would have to wear my gold pieces taped to my body." She glanced again at Jane, and the lowering of her eyelids seemed to say, "Jane, it's your turn."

"Daddy." Jane turned her face to him. "Aunt Matilda has done so much for us. What if I accompanied her to Hawaii?"

His mouth fell open. After several moments, he closed it. He opened it again. "Jane, you're getting married."

CHAPTER 4

Jane could say one thing with confidence. "Daddy, you know I can't have anyone but Aunt Matilda plan my wedding. She's been like a mother to me." She lowered her hands to her lap and absently moved the diamond ring toward her knuckle and back again. "We can't expect her to plan a wedding while her sister-in-law is . . ."

Instead of finishing the sentence, she looked down at her food. A sense of guilt washed over her for having felt so excited over the possibility of going to Hawaii when the situation was so dire. But Matilda's phrase *paradise in the Pacific* kept tripping across her mind.

"Daddy," she said, "Aunt Matilda has done so much for us. For me. Maybe it's time we did something for her."

He certainly couldn't dispute that. Matilda kept her eyelids demurely lowered and her napkin pressed to her lips.

Her dad was rarely without words, but he seemed to be searching for some. Finally he said, "Matilda, you don't know how long you'd be away."

She shook her head. "No. There's no way of knowing."

He exhaled heavily. "Jane, what would Austin say about your being away for . . ." He shrugged. "An indefinite period of time?"

"Why, Daddy," she said as if mortified. "Austin spent those years away from me getting his education. Should he have that privilege, but not me because I'm a woman? Would you want me to marry a man so selfish that he wouldn't want me to be a kind, caring person?"

He seemed to be struggling with how to answer. Finally he said, "Well no, of course not."

"Oh Buck," Matilda said, drawing his attention back to her. "Pansy wrote several years ago that the tourist trade has started in Hawaii. By the hundreds, people from all over the world visit each year. It's a paradise, Buck. Why, it wouldn't surprise me if Jane decided to get married there. It's a perfect place for a honeymoon."

Matilda made it sound like everything was settled. She had included the romantic idea of a wedding and honeymoon in spite of her sister-in-law's illness. But looking from her aunt to her dad, Jane recognized that uncertain look in his eyes. He frowned. "I've heard it's an uncivilized place."

"Uncivilized? Why, Buck, it's been seventy years since the missionaries went there and made the Hawaiians wear clothing." Matilda's hand came up and lay against the bodice of her dress, fashioned in the latest style. "And too," she went on. "Pansy said they've almost stamped out those sensuous hula dances. The hula is only done now for parties and special occasions, and the dancers wear clothes." She fanned her face with her hand as if the thought were too heated to discuss.

Jane stole a glance at Pilar. The two of them had seen Matilda's own version of the hula right in Jane's bedroom.

"Why, those Hawaiians don't even square dance like you do here in Texas."

Jane could almost visualize Matilda teaching the Hawaiians to square dance. Her dad was probably thinking the same thing.

Matilda must have seen his brow furrow and the slight shake of his head. She moved to another subject. "Besides Buck, from information I've received from Pansy, Hawaii is so civilized they don't let their cows wander off unattended right up in their front yards. Her gaze moved to the wide windows of the dining room, as if seeing a herd of cows.

Her dad's gaze followed Matilda's, and he spoke defensively. "They have to graze."

"Yes Buck, but not so close to the house. Why, Pansy said the cattle and horse ranches there had cowboys before we had them here."

"Hawaii has cowboys?"

Matilda nodded. "Hawaii has huge cattle ranches, and Pansy said the cowboys are called *paniolos*. They send salted beef all over the world. Apparently, their ranchers are as advanced as — or perhaps more advanced than — you are here." She paused, giving him time to take that in. Jane and Matilda knew her dad did everything in the most up-to-date way.

Matilda went further. "Jane and I could check that out and send information to you. Besides," she added, "A spirited girl like Jane needs an adventure before she settles down to take care of a man for the rest of her life. Austin has said he had enough travel during his years abroad. He wants to settle down."

Jane watched her father's face. He seemed to be in deep thought. She knew he loved her, but ever since she had turned thirteen, he hadn't quite known what to do with her except treat her like he would a boy. She was grateful for that and for Matilda's influence on her life. Because they never tamed her wild streak, Jane did not consider herself a drawing room type of person.

"Jane, what about your students?" her dad said in an apparent last-ditch effort to find a reason not to let her go.

"Daddy, they are equestrian students," she said, as if he were the child and she the parent. "The classes are at my convenience and theirs."

His eyes brightened. "Your own equestrian events, Jane. You're becoming a well-established equestrienne."

Jane tried not to show the sudden stab of disappointment that swept over her like a cloud of Texas wind in a dust storm. In the last two events, she'd placed second to Rebecca Cawdell. It was downright embarrassing every time she looked at the trophy or anyone congratulated her.

"Well, if they're advanced in Hawaii like Aunt Matilda says, I could learn even more while I'm there." Maybe she really could and come back to get that gloating gleam out of Rebecca's eyes.

Although he smiled before he said, "I

would miss you," he sounded sad.

Jane reached over and covered his hand with hers. "Daddy, you could come there any time. Even go with us, if you like."

His lips tightened, but she saw the slight glimmer in his eyes meaning that such an event was a real possibility.

"Of course you could," Matilda said. "Buck, I couldn't very well have asked you to come along unless Jane agreed first. But that would be wonderful, having Jane and you along on this most important trip to be with my poor, ailing sister-in-law and comfort my brother."

That brought it back around to the seriousness of the trip.

Jane did want to be helpful to the Russells. She expected, however, that she and Matilda would still be able to see the sights of that exotic land. But how much freedom would she have with her father there watching her every move?

CHAPTER 5

Jane picked at her meal. The delicious aroma had vanished, and the food was tasteless. She could not pressure her father into anything. Matilda was the only person in the world who could come close to talking back to him and get away with it.

And too, Matilda had taught her that more flies are caught with sugar than with vinegar. So Jane sat there being sweet.

"Well," her dad said, "I realize this is important to you, Matilda. And Jane . . ." Straightening his shoulders he leaned back against the chair, a signal that he had decided.

"Jane," he said, "since you will have to wait until your aunt returns before the wedding is planned, and if it's what you want . . ."

Jane nodded and lowered her eyes lest they pop out with anticipation.

"This trip can be a wedding present from

me. That way, apart from the sadness of the situation, you may find some joy in your journey."

Her heart hammered against her chest. "I really think it's something I should do, Daddy."

"Yes," he said. "I can tell both you and Matilda feel a great sense of responsibility in this matter." His glance swung toward the high ceiling. She had the feeling he might understand her and Matilda better than she'd realized.

"But with you gone, that would mean changes here, too. Eating dinner alone without my little girl. For a year, at least."

His gaze wandered to Pilar. Was he thinking he wouldn't need Pilar and her mother without Jane around? But how could he in all good conscience dismiss them, even for a year, after he'd saved them from a life of destitution?

Her father seemed to be debating the issue himself. "Matilda will be busy comforting her brother." He smiled at Matilda, then turned his attention back to Jane. "You might become bored."

Bored? Jane could hardly believe that word. The stories from Pansy's letters that Matilda had shared over the years had been enchanting. Of course, Matilda had a way

36

of making a trickle of water sound like an oil gusher.

Matilda slapped both hands down on the table and put on her best smile. "You are so right, Buck. Why not send along a companion for Jane?"

"Wha—" Jane's father stammered. "Who?"

"Why, who else but the one you implied." She lifted her hands in the air. "Pilar."

Pilar screamed, and they all jumped.

She quickly slapped her hand against her mouth, and the gulp of swallowing just about made her choke.

A face peered around the dining room doorway. Jane glanced from Inez to Pilar, whose head began to bob like it might fall from her neck. Her mother's head was doing the opposite, moving from side to side as if the very idea was out of the question.

Jane knew that Pilar was happy just pulling down the bedcovers for Matilda. The thought of going to Hawaii would be as earthshaking to her as it was to Jane.

"Daddy, Pilar has been very much like a companion to me — at times like a younger sister." That was partly true. In earlier years, they had cried together about Pilar's loss of her dad.

"Besides Buck," Matilda said, looking at Inez instead of him. "Inez is capable of running this household without Pilar. I mean, with only . . . you here."

Inez's hand moved to the throat of her high-necked black dress. "But she's only seventeen."

"Oh how lovely." Matilda about came out of her chair. "Imagine Pilar celebrating her coming-out debut in Hawaii."

She'd shocked them all into taking on the demeanor of statues. After a long moment, the unblinking gaze of Inez moved to Pilar. The two stared at each other as if looking at strangers.

Jane wondered if Inez was thinking about a coming-out debut. When Inez's husband had lost his business and killed himself, it had seemed that any hope of Pilar's marrying into a fine family was gone.

Inez turned and disappeared from the dining room. Pilar's head was bent, not bobbing anymore, and her teeth had captured her lower lip.

Matilda sighed. "Maybe I can convince Inez to let Pilar go as a companion to Jane."

After dinner Jane walked with Matilda in the gardens, and they settled on a bench.

"Matilda, what was the tragedy Pansy mentioned?"

Her aunt paused. "I honestly don't recall, Jane. We wrote to each other often, and she told about many events in their church and school. The MacCauley name seems familiar, but I just can't place which tragedy that was." She patted Jane's hand. "We can find out when we get there."

When they got there. Oh, she could hardly wait. And she could hardly believe her dad had given his permission and blessing.

"Matilda, I can't get over how you can get people to do what you want them to. I know why Daddy agreed to send Pilar along." She laughed. "To help protect me. But Inez was shaking her head with that stiff look on her face. As soon as you talked with her in the kitchen, though, she relented."

"Didn't you notice, dear?" Matilda said with an air of superiority. "She didn't have much fight left when I reminded her that she and your daddy would be here alone."

Jane wasn't sure she understood.

Matilda grinned. "Inez used to be very friendly with me. But after your mother died, she seemed to be competing with me for your father's attention. I think she's sweet on him."

Jane's mouth opened in surprise. "I never suspected. I don't think he does, either."

Matilda nodded. "She probably tells herself it's gratitude. The Ashcrofts were never extremely well-off, but they were considered successful and were accepted in society circles. After the bankruptcy and the shame of suicide, that vanished. Inez has, not so graciously, accepted her role as housekeeper and has tried to teach Pilar that she is only working class."

"Takes a strong woman to do that, doesn't it?"

"Indeed," Matilda said.

"Um, Matilda, have you been . . . are you . . . sweet on my daddy?"

Matilda laughed. "My dear, if I were, don't you think I'd have had him proposing to me by now?"

Jane giggled. "Well, yes." She had no doubt that Matilda could marry any man she wanted to.

"He's too much like his brother. So . . . settled, I suppose you could say."

"Weren't you happy with Uncle Wesley?"

"Oh, yes. I livened him up, and we traveled all over. But you don't always know what you want or what you're getting until after you've got it." Her eyebrows lifted. "Don't you worry about Austin." She smiled off into the trees. "You'll liven him up."

Realizing she was twisting the ring on her finger, Jane looked down. Traveling to Hawaii and back would take about ten months, at least. They couldn't just get there and turn around and come right back. Possibly for more than a year, she wouldn't have to be concerned about planning or even thinking about a wedding. Just as Austin's travels had settled him, so would hers.

When she returned, she'd be ready for that . . . surely.

She dared not look at Matilda. Burning deep inside her and making vivid pictures in her mind was that island of paradise. Like a jewel in the sea on the blue Pacific, it seemed to sparkle in her mind with a brilliance far greater than what she wore on her finger.

CHAPTER 6

Before Mak could dismount at the mission school, Reverend Russell ran out of his house across the street and rushed up to him. Mak's first thought was that Pansy had died. But the reverend wore a wide smile, and his eyes were brighter than Mak had seen in a while. Maybe he was going to say one of those phrases like his wife was now in heaven with Jesus. If he did, Mak would turn Big Brown around and have him gallop back to the ranch.

Although it likely would be true, no man had a right to be glad his wife had died. He braced himself. The reverend waved a pink piece of paper at him. "Mak! Mak! My sister is coming to the island."

"Your sister," Mak repeated for lack of anything more to say.

"Yes, yes. Come on. Get down from there and look at this."

Mak dismounted and took his class materials from his saddlebag. He passed the reins to a schoolboy, who ran out to lead the horse out back and tie him in the shade where he could have feed and water. After giving the stallion a farewell stroke, Mak looked down at the pink paper.

The way Russell was tapping the paper with his finger prevented Mak from reading it, but the man looked up at him above his half-glasses and told him what was in it.

"This was written the week before they planned to leave port. They could be here within a week. Or sooner depending on how smooth the crossing is."

"They, you said?"

"Ah yes. Matilda, that's my sister's name. Haven't seen her in ten years. She's bringing her niece. Oh, how old is that little girl now? Janie was about thirteen, maybe fourteen last I saw her." He looked off, not seeing children at the door of the school but a memory tucked in his mind.

"Janie was a skinny little thing. Orange pigtails. Big eyes and a face full of freckles." He sighed and looked at the ground as if he'd returned to reality. Then he gazed into Mak's eyes. "That was a hard time for her."

Mak could imagine. The description Russell gave left a lot to be desired.

"But Matilda can do anything, Mak.

Doesn't matter if it's a business or a school, she can run it. Why, she could even take over the preaching if need be."

Mak stared at Russell as he chuckled. "Oh, and a companion for Jane. A young woman they took in after —" He folded the paper. "But you don't need to know the details."

Mak could agree with that. The most he needed to know was that someone was coming to help at school and he could get back to his business on the ranch. "How is Miz Pansy today?"

Russell's face brightened. "This has done her a world of good, Mak. We can see where her illness is headed, just like the doctors said. But she'll hang on for Matilda." He nodded. "You just wait and see."

Mak nodded, wondering which was easier — knowing your wife was going to die or experiencing the unexpected shock of it. He focused his gaze on a wagonload of children being drawn up to the school, grateful for any distraction from his disturbing thoughts.

With a finger movement toward his hat, Mak left the reverend and walked toward the long, two-story school, as many children were now doing. Lessons would begin soon.

Greeting children while walking across the long porch, he was again reminded that some were as young as Leia. Was it fair to turn his mother into a teacher? She was already a substitute mother. He wasn't sure anymore . . . about many things.

After morning classes, Mak returned to the ranch, and Leia ran out to meet him as usual. After dismounting, he knelt to take her in his arms. He hardly felt her soft little arms around his neck before she moved back and began asking a zillion questions.

"Is Miss Pansy any better? What did you teach? Can you teach me what you teached them? Put me up there and let me ride. You can hold me real tight and I won't fall off."

The last time Mak had tried that at her request, she'd screamed no at the last minute, and he'd visualized the horrible scene all over again and felt the emotion of it. Yes, he understood his little girl wanting something she couldn't have. He had lived that way for three years.

He nodded to a stable boy who came to lead Big Brown to the barn.

Leia put her hands, balled into little fists, on her sides and poked out her bottom lip.

"Watch out. Your lip might get stuck like that."

She snickered.

He smiled at his little girl, aware of her beauty like her mother's. Black curls and eyes so dark they often looked black. Her skin was a smooth, deep, tan color typical of Tahitians.

His mother often said Leia resembled her mother in coloring but was like him in stubbornness.

"I'll tell you all about school at dinner," he said. "I need to check on Panai."

He saw the droop of her little shoulders when she turned toward the porch. He didn't look into his mother's eyes but felt her stare. Maybe someday he could shake that feeling of tension that he didn't measure up to what his mother wanted of him.

After finding out how things went at the ranch and apologizing to Panai for not being around him all day, he cleaned up and joined his mother and daughter for dinner.

His mother gave thanks, and then she and Leia bombarded him with questions about the visitors, most of which he was unable to answer.

"Reverend Russell did say that one of the visitors had orange hair and freckles." He hoped to prepare Leia so she wouldn't be too surprised upon seeing the reverend's guest and blurt out something to hurt her feelings. She'd been raised with people of different nationalities and coloring, so she had no problems with that. But he didn't think either of them had seen anyone with orange hair.

He watched the twitching of Leia's lips as if she wondered how to deal with that. Her little shoulders fell as she exhaled deeply and began to eat. His mother's eyebrows arched, but she changed the subject.

"You seem to enjoy teaching at the school."

Was that a note of pride in her voice? Had he finally pleased her?

"Believe me, teaching horses is a lot easier than teaching such energetic children. They are a challenge. But yes," he said. "I find it fulfilling. I'm glad to be of service to society the same as anyone else." He sighed. "I know you would like to help, Mother. And you could do it better than I. But I need you here with Leia."

Her silence spoke as loud as her words. He, or she, could take Leia along.

"Daddy, what's their name?"

"Who? The children?"

She held up three fingers. "The one-two-three new ones that's coming on a ship."

"Matilda, I think. And Janie. I don't recall his saying the name of the other one."

"How old are they?"

"Well, Matilda is Reverend Russell's sister, so she would likely be about his and your grandmother's age. Janie. Let's see." He looked into his memory. "Reverend Russell said he saw her ten years ago and she was thirteen or fourteen, so she should be twenty-three or twenty-four. The other one is a companion, so she wouldn't be a child. But I don't know if she's young or old."

"This Jane must be single," his mother said, as if she were not thinking of someone for him. But she was always thinking of someone for him. "I mean, coming this far with a companion and not a husband."

Mak shrugged. He wouldn't know. But it's possible that being an orange-haired woman with eyes big as a crocodile's and a splotched face might be reason enough for still being single at that age. He immediately chided himself for the unkind thought. People couldn't help their outer appearance any more than they could help what fate dealt them.

"Daddy, can we meet them at the dock?"

His grimace made the hope on her face wane.

It was a great treat of most islanders — going to the dock, greeting newcomers and visitors, seeing how they dressed, what they brought with them, finding out if they were going to stay.

"These are Reverend Russell's relatives,"

his mother said. "I can't imagine that we wouldn't go." Her eyes questioned, or perhaps challenged, Mak. But she waited for his reply.

He nodded. "Doesn't everyone go to the docks when ships come in?"

Leia squealed and clapped her hands. Ah, he'd made the women in his life happy . . . for the moment. "Can we make leis for them?" She glanced from him to his mother, looking for approval. "They're coming to help Miss Pansy. And Miss Pansy is my special friend."

"That's a wonderful idea," he said.

For the next several days, they took as much interest in those leis as he did his horses. His mother and Leia were making three leis of shells, beads, seeds, and feathers. Greeters would bring fresh flowers to the dock. Those could be added to any kind of lei the moment a ship appeared as a dot on the horizon.

"You two are doing a fine job," he said. His mother and daughter looked like he'd given them a piece of heaven when he added, "Reverend Russell said his sister has been a teacher and that her niece has finished college, and one or both will probably take over for me in the classroom. Leia, when the new teachers come, I will think about letting you go to their school."

He'd pleased his family and told himself he would seriously consider it. Pansy's sister-in-law and niece would likely have the same sweet, loving, gentle nature that Pansy had.

CHAPTER 7

October 1889, Hawaii

"Focus on the horizon," Jane and the other passengers were told by the captain. "That will get you accustomed to solid ground again. Just like you had to get your sea legs, you'll now have to get your land legs back."

Jane didn't worry about that. She was ready for land. During those first few days of travel, she had taken care of the others, putting cold cloths on Matilda's and Pilar's heads when they had come down with bad cases of seasickness.

Now she stood at the railing, focused on the horizon for that first glimpse of land. Once it first appeared like a pencil line across the ocean, it always reappeared no matter how high the waves.

"Like oil," Jane said, glancing at the faces of Matilda and Pilar, who looked as excited as she felt. "No matter how much water, the oil keeps rising to the top."

"And often looks like a rainbow of color," Matilda said.

"Speaking of rainbows, look." A rainbow of colors more vivid than she had ever imagined made a halo over the ocean and that speck of land.

So this was her first glimpse of Hawaii. Swept away like an ocean wave was any concern or fatigue of that long, wearisome, boring, sometimes perilous voyage.

A sparkling deep blue sea splashed up against high, jagged rocks. As they drew nearer, mountainsides of brilliant green appeared, then palm trees. Their tall, slender trunks rose into the clearest blue sky she'd ever seen. The tops of the trees were crowned by fan-shaped leaves, reminding her of peacocks proudly spreading their tail feathers.

"Oh, that aroma," Jane said.

Matilda laughed. "It's certainly not of cattle droppings and horses."

Jane and Pilar laughed, too. As much as Jane enjoyed the smell of horses, she was delighted with this mixture of heady yet delicate flower scents. She'd never thought about smelling an island. She supposed travelers to Texas might think it had the odor of cattle and oil.

"Oh look," Pilar said, pressing her hand

against her heart. "They're getting into canoes and coming out here. Are they —" Her face screwed up like a tight fist. "Are they going to attack us?"

"Of course not." Matilda scoffed.

Pilar wasn't convinced. "Mr. Buckley said they're uncivilized. And Miss Matilda, in our history lessons on the way over here, you said they killed Captain Cook."

Matilda scoffed again. "You would have failed if I had given you a test on it, Pilar. That was more than a hundred years ago. And the people thought he was a god and couldn't die. I doubt they're going to think we are gods." She laughed.

Jane smiled and looked out at the big brown men, their muscles bulging as they rowed, moving through the water faster than the ship. "Aunt Matilda," she said timidly. "Those men are wearing skirts and necklaces."

Matilda patted Jane's hand that was clinging to the ship's railing. "Those are costumes, dear. Pansy wrote about them. These men are greeters. They don't always dress like that. I didn't tell you because I didn't want to spoil the surprise. And those things around their necks are not called necklaces. Pansy wrote me all about it. Those are . . ." She stood thoughtful for a moment, holding her hat against the sudden swift breeze. "Pansy spelled it l-e-i-s. I suppose they're called lee-eyes."

"Aloha, Aloha, Komo mai," the rowers called. The passengers waved and yelled, "Hello and thank you."

"Don't they speak English?" Jane asked.

"Pansy said English is the official language," Matilda said. "But they like to give a Hawaiian greeting."

The rowers escorted the boat to the wharf, where passengers disembarked down the gangway. They pulled the canoes up onto the white sand and formed a border, making a path for the passengers to walk through, each one bowing, greeting. Jane saw then that the "lee-eyes" the greeters wore seemed to be made of shells and what looked like long teeth and pieces of bone.

At first, Jane thought there must be some personage of high acclaim aboard ship, even though she thought she'd met all the passengers. The welcomes and greetings, however, seemed to be for each of them. At the end of the row of men stood many women and groups of children. The women came forward and greeted each of them as if they were long-lost friends.

"Matilda. Is that you?" A man in a suit came up to them.

Matilda screeched, "Russ!"

Jane feared her aunt would break his body with her exuberant hug. However, he wasn't a small man and seemed quite strong. He looked slightly older than Matilda, and his thin brown hair had a lot of gray in it. They broke apart, and she kissed his cheeks and he kissed hers. Both had tears in their eyes.

Matilda stood shaking her head like it was all unbelievable. Finally her brother wiped at his eyes and looked away from her. "Is this little Janie?"

Jane nodded and went into his open arms. Then he held her away by the shoulders. "You're not little anymore."

What could she say? "Ten years does that to a girl."

He laughed. "And it did it well. Ah, this is Pilar?"

She said, "Yes sir," and he opened his arms to her.

Uncle Russ motioned to a group of people. A woman and a little girl hurried up to them. Jane was surprised they wore clothing much like one would wear in Texas. But that healthy-looking woman couldn't be Pansy.

"Matilda," her uncle Russell said, "meet a dear friend, Rose MacCauley."

"Oh I'm so anxious to get to know you,"

the woman said. She held up a long loop of flowers and managed, in spite of the big hat, to slip it over Matilda's head and make sure it draped equally down her back and chest.

"Jane, this is Leia MacCauley," Uncle Russ said with a big smile. The child reached up for Jane, who bent down and for some strange reason felt like she might topple to the ground. However, as the child was arranging the loop as Rose had done for Matilda, Jane said, "Thank you, Leia, for the 'lee-eye.' "

The girl wrinkled her nose. "What's a 'lee-eye'?"

Uh-oh. Jane felt like an excessive amount of saliva had formed under her tongue. Something wasn't right. The people around her began to sway. "This . . . this necklace is called . . . what?"

"It's a lei," Leia said and snickered. She pronounced it *lay*. To make matters worse, the child turned to a man several feet away, standing with a group of children. "Miss Jane called the lei a 'lee-eye,' Daddy." She put her hand over her mouth.

Children snickered.

Rose MacCauley motioned to the man called Daddy. "Mak, come and meet Russell's relatives."

Jane looked at the ruggedly handsome

man, who lowered his gaze to the ground. She resented what she felt was an unsuccessful attempt to keep a grin off his face. But what could she expect from a man holding in front of him a hat with flowers around the band?

The man came closer. But why was he swaying?

She heard the name. "Mak MacCauley," and somewhere in her swirling mind it registered that he had been mentioned in Pansy's letter as a teacher. But the hat? Was that another lei for her?

Just in case, she said, "I could use a hat like that."

He said abruptly without a smile, "Sorry I can't say the same about yours."

Should she laugh? Be insulted?

No, he must be drunk. He couldn't stand still. In fact, he often seemed to be twins. Looking around at the others, she saw that they too became like waves on an ocean.

She had that excessive saliva feeling again, and her ocean waves were not gently rolling but sloshing against her insides. She had to swallow it, but something wouldn't go down. Instead, that something was coming up.

Aboard ship they'd been warned it might take a while to get their land legs back, and if they felt dizzy, they should hold onto something. She extended her hand. Mak did the same. But before they could touch, she withdrew hers and covered her mouth with her gloved hand.

She heard some exclamations and Matilda's voice. "Oh, my dear. We were told that green is even greener in Hawaii, but I didn't know they meant faces. You look perfectly ghastly."

Jane could only focus on what was in front of her, and she stared in horror at the man who stared back, making her feel like the most disgusting creature in the world. She should have kept her focus on the horizon. "I feel . . . I feel . . . I . . . uh . . ."

She turned and ran.

CHAPTER 8

Jane made it a few feet behind a bench to a grassy spot and felt like a cow heaving in labor. She colored the grass even greener with whatever had been inside her stomach. She wiped her mouth with a . . . silk bandana?

Bent over, the lei swinging in front of her, she managed to look around and up to the side and saw the man with the flowered hat now on his head and minus a bandana around his neck.

"Thank you," she managed to squeak out after wiping her mouth. Looking down she didn't see anything unseemly on the lei or on her clothes. Straightening she accepted the arm he offered and allowed herself to be led to a bench. She took a deep breath but only exhaled through her nose lest he guess what had soured in her stomach.

Leia came over and pulled a little purse from her pocket. "Don't feel bad." She wrinkled her nose distastefully. "People do it all the time."

Jane noticed that several other passengers were doing exactly that. Some had been fortunate enough to find a reasonably private place to empty their stomachs. Matilda and Pilar gave her sympathetic grins.

"This will help," the little girl said, holding out a piece of hard candy.

Although she feared having anything in her stomach, Jane accepted the candy. Maybe it would at least freshen her breath enough that she could again join the others.

"Thank you," she whispered to the girl, who smiled and said, "Are you the new teacher?"

Jane didn't know what Pastor Russell's needs might be, but there was no way in the world she was going to be a teacher confined to a school building. Her hesitation was filled by Matilda coming over. "Can you walk, dear? We need to get you someplace where you can lie down."

"Oh no," Jane said, rising from the bench. She held the soiled bandana in one gloved hand and placed the other hand on Matilda's arm. "I think standing still is what did it." As they walked up to Uncle Russell and Rose, she apologized. Matilda had said her face had been green. She felt sure it had turned deathly white from the way she had felt. Now feeling warm, her face was probably red.

She laughed. "Oh, I must be a sight."

"Oh, you're fine." Rose MacCauley echoed Leia's words. "It's not unusual. A voyage like that is hard on a person. Believe me, I know."

Jane tried to smile, but even that effort felt weak. She was trying to figure out the relationships here. The man, woman, and child were MacCauleys. The woman looked older than the man, but she was quite lovely.

She didn't feel it proper to ask. Anyway, Matilda was still discussing her. "Jane was never seasick a moment aboard ship. She had her sea legs the whole time. We decided that must have been due to her being such an avid horseback rider."

"Avid?" Rose MacCauley said as if that were shocking. The woman's eyes widened as she looked from Matilda to Jane and back again.

Jane saw the questioning flicker in Matilda's eyes. Like she, Matilda must be wondering if the woman was asking the meaning of the word.

After a moment of hesitation, Matilda simply said, "Yes. Our Jane is an expert equestrienne."

Mak's mother put her hand to her heart. "Another example that God brings good from the worst of things."

Jane didn't exactly follow her line of reasoning. Perhaps the woman hadn't understood the words *avid* or *equestrienne.*

Rose MacCauley turned to the man who had stepped aside. "Mak," she said. "It might help if Jane rode your horse. She's not ready for land yet."

Jane thought he looked dumbfounded. He snorted, not like a horse, but it was definitely a snort. "You know the horse is spirited. And . . ." He gestured toward her. "Miz . . ."

Jane knew he didn't remember her name. He changed his wording. "She wouldn't know where to go."

"Then perhaps you could give her a ride," the woman said in a low but meaningful tone.

Pushing the candy aside with her tongue, Jane took several gulps of air. "I'll be all right. I don't think there's anything left in me." Looking around at the men in skirts she saw pants legs exposed beneath the flowered material wrapped around their thighs. "Maybe I could go for a canoe ride or something."

Matilda seemed to like the idea. "Oh, wouldn't that be fun."

"No, no," Uncle Russell said, shaking his head vigorously. "I don't recommend that. But Mak," he said to the man, who had stepped farther away from them. "A ride might be a good idea. The schoolchildren are too excited for lessons. You could take Janie to my house, and she could get some ginger tea. You'd be there before our carriages or the children in the wagons."

"It's all right," she said, seeing his frown and knowing the man didn't want her on his horse. Or did he just not want her near him?

As if confirming that, he turned and walked away, past the children toward where a couple of wagons tied to horses were in the shade. Uncle Russell offered an arm, and Jane began to move toward a carriage. "Oh," she said, "this is like walking on marshmallows."

Next thing she knew, a huge brown stallion was right beside her. The man with the flowered hat reached down for her.

"You don't have to do this."

"I know," he said. Uncle Russell put his hands on her waist and helped hoist her up. Oh what she'd do for riding pants right now. However, she squished her billowing skirts

63

around her to keep them away from the horse's head and from being able to fly up and blind this . . . person . . . who wore flowers.

The man had his arms around her, holding on to the reins, looking over her head, and she was breathing the most wonderful sweet air and feeling the cool breeze on her face. They were only trotting, but the movement was similar to being aboard ship. Her shoulder was pressed into his flowered shirt.

She ventured a glance at him. He saw it and said, "Try not to throw up on my horse."

A deep breath of air filled her chest, and she felt her shoulders rise with it. She was well enough to remember someone had called him Mak. That was the name of the person Matilda had said was teaching for Pansy.

That little girl had asked if Jane would be her teacher. Well, she figured she would be as qualified as this aloof man. She would not just sit there and let him make fun of her, even if she did feel much more comfortable and hardly aware of any surroundings other than the strong arms around her and the musky smell of him combined with that of flowers . . . on his hat.

"I wouldn't insult a horse by throwing up

on him," she said. Noticing the pocket on his shirt, she reached up and pulled at it gently with her gloved finger. "I could just deposit it right here."

CHAPTER 9

Equestrienne? That's what the woman had
said of this sassy young woman who
wouldn't surprise him if she did throw up
in his pocket. Perhaps her horseback training made her sit so straight. Or was it his
reluctant attitude that rankled her into that
erect posture? On second thought, he
doubted that. After all, she had accepted
the ride.

He felt it best not to attempt small talk.
While he kept glancing at her hair beneath
her hat to determine just how orange it
might be, she kept her eyes on the scenery,
which was not too inspiring at the dock.

Whether this would be simply a ride for a
couple miles to the area where the mission
house, school, and Reverend Russell's house
were located would depend upon her reaction. If she began to thank him, compliment him, or any other of that female kind
of thing, he'd gallop her right up to the

reverend's home and deposit her.

He left the dock area and trotted the horse along the beach where she could feel the motion and see the ocean. She gasped. "Oh, I've never ridden a horse on a beach."

The turn of her head from one side to the other revealed her wonder as she looked at the ocean, smiled, took deep breaths, and looked up at palm trees.

Seeing her enjoyment and hearing her say, "I'm feeling much better," he rode farther and longer than he'd intended.

The carriages and wagons were already lined up in front of Reverend Russell's home when they arrived. Russell must have heard the horse's hooves when Mak rode up to his house. He came out and reached up for Jane, who then held onto his shoulders and tested her land legs.

"I think I'm okay now," she said. "I feel a little weak, but . . . okay." She looked up at Mak. "Thank you," she said softly, but her eyes, which were not big as a crocodile's but were big enough to be interesting, held a guarded expression as if she didn't know what to think of him.

Good.

He didn't want her thinking of him.

At least her face no longer looked green. Not splotched either, although he had

67

observed a few tiny freckles across her nose on otherwise flawless skin. She wasn't bad looking. With that hat he couldn't be sure of her hair, but he thought it more a sun gold than orange. And the few strands of her hair that had blown against his face had not come from a fourteen-year-old with her hair in pigtails.

He touched the brim of his hat and gave a slight nod. "I'd be grateful, Reverend," he said, seeing that his mother's carriage was at the side of the house, "if you would please tell Mother and Leia I'll be at home."

The reverend lifted his hand in response before he smiled at Jane and said, "Come inside. We've made some ginger tea for you. That will make you feel better. Maybe you can eat a soda cracker."

Mak turned Big Brown as he saw Jane put her hand on the reverend's arm and heard the man telling her to call him Uncle Russell. She walked with him up on the porch, where Leia came out.

"Are you coming in, Daddy?"

In a house filled with sickness and women and a preacher? "I need to go and check on Panai, Leia. I'll see you at home, later."

She lifted her hand and waved at him, then reached out to take hold of Jane's free hand.

Mak adjusted himself better in the saddle, which felt rather empty now. He didn't like the feeling of remembering when he and Maylea had ridden like that, nor did he like a woman being so close, the feel of his arms around her. Nobody should have been on this horse with him. It only made him miss Maylea even more.

Of course the feeling had nothing to do with Jane; she had simply brought out emotions that were never far from the surface. He had nothing against her. He just didn't need any woman invading his space.

Mak galloped the horse faster than usual, needing the wind on his face. He longed to feel free, to ride until all the distress was blown from him. It never happened. But he spent the rest of the afternoon tending to Panai, where his hope lay. Later he spent time in the ring with the wild mustang he was in the process of taming. Being in control of something was a good feeling.

Hearing the clanging of the triangle, he had Kolani take the mustang into the stables. After washing up, he entered the kitchen as Coco was putting dinner on the table.

His mother's blessing seemed shorter than usual.

"First," he said, upon seeing Leia's eyes

69

light up and knowing she was about to go into a long spill about the day's events, "before you tell all about the reverend's relatives, how was Miz Pansy today?"

"Oh, so much better, Daddy. She just smiled and cried. She said they were happy tears."

"I'm sure they were, honey."

"Pansy has hung on for this, Mak," his mother said. "She was so happy. But you know she's been getting weaker."

"Miss Jane got better." Leia's eyes widened. "She might could be my teacher if I could go to school. I like her, Daddy." Her little shoulders lifted with her deep breath. "And I like Miss Pilar. She's nice. And Miss Tilda, oh my."

His mother laughed.

Mak glanced from one to the other. "Now what does that mean?"

Leia shook her head, and her gaze traveled around as if she were trying to see an answer. "I don't know," she said. "But I think . . . oh, I know. Miss Tilda is like a volcano."

They all laughed. He had taken Leia close enough to see the fire that continually spouted up like a fountain, lighting up a night sky with red fireworks, literally.

"Oh she is, Mak," his mother agreed. "She

70

is so full of life. I think we're friends already."

"Me, too," Leia assured them. "And Miss Jane and Miss Pilar are my friends. Miss Jane might could be my teacher. I'm cleaning up my plate."

Sure . . . that should do it.

His mother turned to him. "Oh Mak. Jane is the one."

"Mother, please," Mak protested. "My one is gone."

"Oh, I don't mean for you." Her laugh sounded like a scoff. "She's the one for Leia. She teaches . . ."

He missed whatever she said next, but he was aware what she had said was a switch. At every ship docking, particularly the tourist ones, she would tell him of beautiful women, and because she was a generous woman, she invited most of them to their home. So now that one appeared who did get his attention by being green and obnoxious, she'd changed her mind about finding him a woman?

"Why is this one not for me?"

His mother smiled. "Oh, Miss Jane was modest about it, but Matilda blurted out the whole thing. Jane has been engaged to marry an oil tycoon's son since the day she was born."

Mak found that puzzling. "I didn't know arranged marriages went on in America."

"Oh, she doesn't have to do it. It's just that her daddy is a wealthy cattle rancher and has been friends with the oil tycoon family forever." She waved her hand in the air and smiled broadly. "So you don't have to worry about me trying to fix you up with this one, or about her being out to get you. She's spoken for."

"Good," he said and kept eating.

She wasn't finished. "And you don't have to worry about her being after your money. Her daddy and her fiancé are filthy rich." She looked at Leia. "Not filthy-dirty. That's just an expression."

Leia nodded and said seriously, "I need to go to school and learn things like that."

"Yes, you do," his mother said and looked triumphantly at him. "Did you see that girl's ring?"

"What girl?"

"Miss Jane."

"I think she was wearing gloves, and I think she might have thrown up on them."

"Well, she didn't hurt the ring. That diamond is big as . . . as . . ."

Leia stuck her hand out over her plate. "As big as a whooooole finger."

His mother's eyebrows lifted. "Close," she

conceded.

This was a welcome change. As his mother said, he wouldn't have to worry about her being after his money, and she was engaged to be married. He needn't give her a moment's thought. He wouldn't need to make a point of keeping his distance.

Perhaps her fiancé would arrive. He understood his mother's excitement over having some new women to talk with, to find out about America. Just as Mak's mother enjoyed the friendship of women who visited Hawaii from other countries, he enjoyed interaction with men.

Mak was beginning to feel good about the situation when Leia said, "Daddy, I'm going to ask the Little People to make Miss Jane be my teacher."

CHAPTER 10

"How are you feeling, dear?" Matilda asked when she and Jane walked out of Reverend Russell's two-story white clapboard house after having a light supper in Uncle Russell's kitchen. They stood on the porch.

"Ashamed," Jane said, taking hold of the banister.

Matilda scoffed. "What in the name of wild horses do you have to be ashamed of?"

Jane groaned. "Oh Matilda. After seeing Aunt Pansy so frail, I realize all my fuss about getting sick was wrong. I have nothing to complain about."

Matilda scoffed. "Oh yes, you do. We're puny little human beings who have enough of the divine in us to want everything to be perfect. I think God put that in us so we'd keep trying to be better people."

Looking at the warmth in Matilda's smile reminded Jane of just how precious that woman was. On the outside she was all fire and energy, but inside she was a million times more valuable than those gold pieces she carried around in the purse against her bosom.

"Pansy cared about how you were feeling," Matilda said softly.

"I know, and that makes me feel bad. The attention should not have been focused on me."

"Oh honey. We all told our seasick stories. Even Pansy joked about never being able to leave Russ because she'd be too seasick going back to Boston. We were all trying to make you feel better."

"I know. And the laughing brought on Pansy's awful coughing spell, and we had to get out of there so the nurse could take care of her."

"But that was good for her. The coughing helps clear her lungs so she can breathe better."

"Maybe you're right."

"Maybe?"

Seeing Matilda take a step away and plant her hands on her hips, Jane laughed. "Okay, you are right."

"I really am in this, Jane." Matilda stepped up next to her and placed her hands on the banister, displaying her jewels and causing Jane to be aware of the single ring she wore, the diamond that sealed her commitment to Austin.

Matilda must have noticed she was looking at the ring. "That is a beautiful diamond, Jane."

"Yes, I know."

"Are you missing Austin?"

Missing him? Austin had always been in her life, and she'd accepted the fact he always would be. She didn't really take anyone for granted after her mother died, but she accepted that both her dad and Austin were there for her.

She supposed people missed those who were absent when they'd been used to their presence. She'd missed Austin when he went away to college. Then she'd missed him when she went to college. She missed him after he joined his dad in the oil business.

So she looked at Matilda's waiting face and said, "Sure. Now that you mention it. I miss Austin and Daddy and Texas. Even Inez."

Matilda smiled and patted her hand, the one with the ring on its finger.

Jane looked at the rose blue sky that was fast turning to magenta. "Like you always told me, Matilda. Life is full of wonderful adventures, and that's where we need to focus our attention — never brooding about what we don't have."

"That's right, Jane. Russ has told us of Pansy's rapid spiral downward, yet she has stayed alive to see us. She so enjoyed this evening. But she's ready for her adventure into eternity."

"So we'll just make her as happy as we can." Jane tapped the banister for emphasis. "Later we can focus on . . . adventure."

"Exactly."

Jane sighed. Well then, she never should have taken that unexpected adventure of a horseback ride on the beach with that sullen cowboy. But that was different. He hadn't wanted her on that horse, and if she hadn't been queasy, she wouldn't have ridden with him. But . . . no more adventures. She would be right here for Pansy and Uncle Russell.

For the next few days, the women unpacked and settled into their individual upstairs rooms. A wide porch formed a balcony over the one below.

"I'm surprised, Uncle Russell," Jane said during the lunch that Pilar had prepared for them from food the church members brought in. "You have such a big house. Not that you shouldn't, but I mean . . . I expected it to be more . . ."

"Modest, I think you mean," Matilda interjected.

"I suppose so."

His eyes lit up with a smile. "Pansy and I are blessed. But you see, a preacher and a teacher have a community full of children — and adults, too — who often need a place to stay. But," he explained, "this was a missionary house when it was first built. Four couples lived in it. As time went by, they left, went to other islands, or built their own new homes."

"So you're really living more modestly than those who built new homes, aren't you, Russ?" Matilda said.

"To be honest, sister," he said. "It's not modesty that kept us here. We happen to like it, and it works to our advantage when there's a visiting pastor. Also, we can invite people who come here for a short visit and even have room for Pansy's Bible studies. We don't have to leave and go somewhere else."

Jane had the feeling that was not a lack of modesty or convenience on his or Pansy's part. They wanted to share their faith and whatever they had with others. "Thanks for sharing your home with us," Jane said.

"My pleasure. Each of you is a great blessing, especially to Pansy." His smile at Matilda was affectionate. "Matilda has the best bedside manner of anyone in the world. Many a time, Pansy and I have talked about the poor and downtrodden —"

"Oh Russ," Matilda scoffed. "Let's talk about something uplifting."

Yes, Jane was thinking. Matilda was always the spark of life in any setting. Her telling about her many travels and adventures was better than seeing a stage play. Jane had wanted to be like her for as long as she could remember — at least like the exciting, adventurous side of her.

During the days that followed, Matilda relieved Uncle Russell of his almost constant attention to Pansy by taking turns with him reading to Pansy while she rested. Matilda spent as much time with her sister-in-law as the nurse would allow.

Jane took over the job of accepting the food church members and friends brought in, glad she didn't have to cook it. She took over the dishwashing, something she had rarely done, so she could organize and get the proper dishes back to the right people.

After only a couple of days, Pilar started to the school, resuming her senior year studies.

"What do you like best about it?" Jane

asked her.

Her dark eyes lit up with pleasure. "I've made a friend named Susanne. She wants to know all about America, and I want to know about Hawaii."

Rose MacCauley visited one morning. She and Matilda took a walk together. Jane could tell the two were friends already.

That evening, Jane and Matilda sat in the swing on the porch watching the sun set while Uncle Russell sat by Pansy's bed as he did each night before she took the medication that would make her sleep.

Matilda lightly pushed the swing with the toe of her shoe. "I asked Rose about the MacCauley tragedy."

"What was it?" Jane said. "Or is that confidential?"

"Rose says the whole island knows. Mak's wife was thrown from one of his racehorses. His workers had to keep him from shooting that great horse. If they'd sold it to anyone except the king, Mak probably would have shot the horse and the new owner."

Jane gasped. "He's that violent?" She knew he was about as happy as a cow on its way to the slaughter house.

"No Jane, he's not violent. It's been three years since Mak's wife was killed. And their unborn baby. Rose said he just can't get over it, and if a woman comes near him, he runs in the opposite direction." She sighed. "He's such a good-looking specimen of a man. What a waste." She shook her head. "Apparently, his letting you ride with him on that horse was nothing short of a miracle."

"Well, he didn't have a lot of choice with his mother and Uncle Russell telling him to in front of everybody. I guess I've started off on the wrong foot with him."

Matilda nodded. "Rose said my mentioning your being a horsewoman, it just seemed the thing to do, and Mak was standing aside so she wanted to include him."

"He was quiet on the ride. Cordial, but I got the distinct feeling he'd rather have been elsewhere."

"According to his mother, he would. She says he's trying to pay more attention to Leia, who is becoming quite an observant and outspoken young lady. He came to the dock because they asked him to. She thinks you would be perfect to teach Leia how to ride."

"I would love to teach her." She shrugged. "But I guess he won't be giving me any more rides. Or the time of day, since he might think I'm out to get him."

"Now, there's the irony of this situation.

That ring right there." Matilda reached over and tapped the set with her finger. "That is why he will give you the time of day. You're no threat. You can't get any wrong ideas about him." She leaned back and smiled smugly. "You're already spoken for."

Jane huffed. "So without even knowing me, he thinks I would be out to get him. But my wearing this ring means I'm about as significant as a . . . as a . . . doormat."

"Exactly."

Jane stared at Matilda, who lifted both shoulders and blinked her eyes innocently before focusing on the scenery ahead of them. Jane looked at the magenta sky, wondering if it were really that color or if she might just be seeing red.

CHAPTER 11

Pansy insisted they all go to church on Sunday and leave her at home. Her voice was barely audible because if she spoke in a normal tone, she went into coughing fits. While the nurse said coughing helped clear her lungs, the fits left Pansy visibly weaker.

"If you're needed," the nurse reassured them, "I can run up to the church. After all, that's where the doctor will be."

When she arrived at church, Jane found it interesting to see Japanese, Chinese, Koreans, and members of many other nationalities as well as American and Europeans. Sometimes, walking down the streets in the town of Hilo she felt like a minority. The stares she and Matilda received made her feel like one. She had not, however, met one person who was unfriendly. Well, unless she counted the flower-hatted horseman.

She almost laughed at that. He hadn't been that unfriendly. And he could have ridden off on his horse without her. Come to think of it, why would he even want to come near a woman who threw up in his bandana and threatened to do so in his pocket?

She wondered if he'd be at church, but when Rose and Leia came in and sat behind them, Mak wasn't with them.

Jane preferred to sit in the back where she could see everyone, but Uncle Russell wanted them to sit up front so they could easily be seen when he introduced them.

Uncle Russell had already told them about the construction of the church's walls. They were made of lava rock, three feet thick, bonded together by sand, crushed coral, and oil from kukui nuts. It was more than one hundred feet long, forty-six feet wide, and had a white steeple one hundred feet high.

Although Jane wasn't surprised by the elaborate way the women and men dressed, she was as surprised by the church as she had been by Uncle Russell's house.

"It's a beautiful church. I've never seen anything like it," she said, after turning in her seat to talk with Rose MacCauley.

Matilda agreed. "Well, we don't use lava rock much in American building because the few active volcanoes we have don't erupt very often and are in remote locations. But this is so elaborate."

Rose nodded and smiled, looking very beautiful in her European-style clothes and big hat, under which her dark brown hair was perfectly groomed. "The king donated the land, so the construction had to be the best," she explained. "Soon after the first missionaries came in the early 1800s, the queen became a Christian. She ordered all the sacred images destroyed. That's when the people began to get rid of their false gods and accept Christianity. The places of worship had to be fit for a queen." She smiled. "Or a king."

Before they could say any more, an organist began to play. A well-dressed man led a choir of men and women, and the congregation joined in singing, "O Worship the King."

Rose leaned forward, her face next to Jane and Matilda. "They're not singing about Hawaii's king."

Jane and Matilda smiled at her and at each other. Jane's eyes wandered around the beautiful wooden walls, the middle aisle separating high-backed pews, the tall columns holding up a balcony on each side of the sanctuary.

Soon however, her thoughts focused on Uncle Russell's sermon. She appreciated his straightforward approach, which reminded her of Matilda's way of not skirting the truth. Not that her preacher in Texas did that, but this sermon seemed more personal, something you could take home with you and think about. He talked about a servant's heart, which is what his congregation had been showing in such special ways for many months after Pansy's illness was diagnosed.

"Even a cup of cold water to a thirsty person," he said, "is very significant to our Lord."

His sermon made Jane uncomfortable. She'd always assumed she was useful to God, but she hadn't thought of it in such specific terms before. She supposed these days of watching Matilda and Uncle Russell put Pansy's needs ahead of everything else gave her a different perspective, too. She'd always said she wanted to be just like Matilda, but she'd concentrated on the adventurous side of her aunt.

The next morning, determined to be more useful, she asked if she could read to Pansy for a while. Both Uncle Russell and Matilda later acted as if she'd done a tremendous good and said they had enjoyed having a cup of coffee together and discussing old times when he and Pansy and Matilda and her husband had cooked and fed the needy in the church fellowship hall after a big flood.

Jane knew Matilda was good and generous, but she hadn't realized the extent of her service to the poor and needy until Uncle Russell began bringing it up and Matilda kept trying to change the subject.

Jane decided to take a walk while the doctor was with Pansy. School would be in recess for lunch soon, so she walked to the more secluded spot where the church, surrounded by lush foliage, was located.

She was in the midst of asking God how she might be of more help to Pansy or Uncle Russell when the unexpected sound of horse's hooves approaching her at the corner of the church startled her. She squealed and recoiled. Should she wait to be run over or dive into the bushes and hope for the best?

"Aloha, Miz Buckley," said a masculine voice she recognized with what she thought was a tinge of British accent and something else. She'd heard only three male voices, and this one did not belong to Uncle Russell nor the doctor, who was now with Pansy. Turning her head to the side, she saw a brown boot beneath a breeches-covered leg against a big brown stallion. Before she could lift her gaze higher, Mak MacCauley swung the other leg over the saddle and stood beside her.

He held the reins in one hand and removed his hat. The wind blew his wavy hair toward his face. His eyes held an expression of curiosity. "Is someone behind the bushes?"

He sounded serious. What kind of animals hid in these bushes? Was a fear of that why he and the big stallion had crept up silently until they were almost upon her? Without moving anything but her eyes she looked at the bushes and back at him. She whispered. "I don't think so. Did you see . . . something?"

"No. But you seemed to be talking to the bushes."

Okay, the first time they met, she threw up. Now he saw her talking, apparently, to a bush. "I was talking to God."

"God's behind the bush?" He didn't smile. "Do you think we should step back in case it bursts into flame?"

Chapter 12

Against her will, Jane's mouth dropped open. The man who had been so aloof was cracking a joke? Or was he being sarcastic? Maybe they just didn't speak the same language, but she'd give him the benefit of the doubt.

"If it bursts into flame we could run and jump into the ocean. I suppose God could part the Pacific Ocean as well as part the Red Sea. But . . . that would be an awful long walk to the other side. It took five months in a ship."

He laughed, and she joined in. Maybe his aloofness the day she arrived had simply been concern about her illness.

His smile vanished as if he had laughed in spite of himself. She gestured toward the bushes. "The bushes just happened to be here. Actually, I was thanking God that we arrived while Pansy is still alive and asking how I could be helpful to her."

With a slight nod he said, "That's com-mendable."

She shook her head. "Not really. I think that's what God tells us to be like." She gave a small self-conscious laugh. "I'm afraid I've been quite pampered and spoiled."

He didn't look surprised. Maybe she'd better change the subject. She turned again to face the bushes. "This is very beautiful." She touched a leaf of the huge plant. She'd never seen leaves quite so large or glossy on what must be a bush since it grew on what appeared to be stalks instead of trunks. The leaves were about four inches wide and ranged from one to two feet long, Her gaze moved up to where some of the stalks were twice her height. "What is it?"

"This variety is *Cordyline fruticosa,* a member of the lily family. There are several varieties. But this one," he said, as she felt him watching while she touched one leaf after another, "this is a Ti plant."

"Tea? Oh, you make tea from this?"

"No, no." Mak laughed. "It's spelled *t-i,* and some westerners call it 'Ti' with a long *i.* However, the correct pronunciation sounds like tea. Many of the native Hawai-ians call it 'Ki.' "

"I've never seen a plant like this."

"It has many uses," he said. "The Hawai-

90

ians used to use the leaves for roof thatching, weaving it into sandals, hula skirts, and even rain capes." He touched a large leaf. "In the past and today, the roots can be baked and eaten as a dessert. Food is sometime wrapped in the leaves and cooked. There are many other uses, including medicinal. And," he added, "they're used to ward off evil spirits."

As her face swung around to look at him, she swiped away wisps of hair that the breeze had teased from her roll and blown into her face. "But that wouldn't be why they're planted around a church."

"Are you sure of that?" he teased.

"Well, Pastor Russell said two-thirds of this island is Christian. And he certainly wouldn't use plants to ward off evil." She gave him a doubtful look. "He uses God's Spirit."

"True," Mak said. "But it all depends on who you want to come to church — those who already believe the Christian religion or those who believe the myths and ancient gods. The unbelievers wouldn't come to hear the pastor because they believe in evil spirits. Even some of the Christians hang on to their superstitions."

"How can they be Christians and still be superstitious?"

91

He gave her a look. "Ever hear of walking under a ladder, or a black cat running in front of you?"

"I take your point," she said. "Or breaking a mirror will give you seven years of bad luck." He was a handsome man. "Is wearing flowers on your hat a superstition?"

"No, it just means we have a lot of them here. They represent this island." He shrugged. "Like that one star you have in Texas."

"One star?" Was he crazy?

"Isn't Texas called the Lone Star State?"

"Yes, but that's in the flag. And it's bigger than any star you'll find in the sky." She emphasized that with a slight bob of her head. "Texas certainly has more than one star in the night sky," she said proudly.

He shrugged as if he didn't care. "Most people say there are more stars here than anywhere in the world. And that comes from good sources since Hawaii is made up of peoples from all over the world."

"I'm not sure what a native Hawaiian is," she said. "But you're not, are you?"

"Well, yes and no," he said. "I was born here and raised here for most of my life. But my parents and grandparents on both sides are Scottish. I traveled with my dad to America when I was fourteen, then was sent to Scotland for my university years."

"I'm surprised there are so many nationalities here," she said.

"Many are like the Scots," he said. "If you know our history, we've been without a country and traveled to other places, such as America. My ancestors came here. In fact, a young Scot became friends with the king, married a Hawaiian woman, and their granddaughter became the wife of a king."

"I had no idea," Jane said.

He nodded. "In past years, all the overseers of the sugar plantations were hired from the University of Aberdeen, Scotland's college of agriculture."

Well, he seemed about as proud of Hawaii as she was of Texas. She could see he would be a good teacher, one who liked to explain things.

"And our current princess, Victoria Kaiulani, named after Queen Victoria," he continued, "is the daughter of Archibald Cleghorn, a Scotsman. She is half Scot and half Hawaiian."

Surprised, Jane said, "I've never been taught anything about Hawaii. All I know are a few stories from Pansy's letters to Matilda."

He nodded. "Hawaiian history wasn't written down until long after the missionaries came in the early 1800s and taught the people to read and write. Their history was handed down by them telling their stories throughout the generations."

She would like to learn more but wasn't even sure what to ask him. She started to ask if he missed Scotland, but instead commented, "Apparently you prefer Hawaii."

"It's my home," he said. "The best parts of my life have been spent here."

Looking at his face, she saw the misery appear. As if to shake it off, he seemed to paste a smile on his face, then looked at her hand. "That looks like an engagement ring."

"Yes." She held up her hand.

"Your fiancé must be very understanding to allow you to come on such a lengthy journey without him."

Allow her? Those words took a little thinking. She would need to clear that up. "It was really my dad who I had to ask. He's the one who pays the bills."

"Oh, no," he said, flustered. "I wasn't implying —"

"Oh, I know that. I was just trying to say in a nice way that I did not ask my fiancé if I could come. I simply informed him." He was looking at her strangely. "I think it's after people are married that those conventions are followed."

"Well yes, of course. But I was thinking about the long trip. Do you plan to be here very long? I mean," he said when she gave him a quick glance, "if I'm not being too personal."

"It's not too personal. But I really don't know. We'll be here as long as Pansy is alive. And as long as Uncle Russell needs us."

"Mmm." He was now nodding at the ground.

"But," she said, lifting her chin, "it wouldn't surprise me if Austin and my dad popped up at any time. They've never let me out of their sight for very long."

"I should think not," he said, and she saw a little color come into his tanned cheeks.

She wondered why he'd stopped. Just to talk to her? In that case . . . "I don't suppose I could take a wee little ride on that horse?" She stood and patted its neck. "I miss mine so much."

The good mood between them vanished. Mak looked like she'd asked him to pull down a star from the sky and give it to her. "I . . . I'm sorry. I must go. My horses need tending. And there's my daughter."

"Sorry," she said. "I didn't throw up on your horse the day I arrived. And I'm fine today. Maybe a tad dizzy upon occasion."

He seemed at a loss for a moment then

gave a short laugh and reached up and patted his pocket. "One can never be sure."

She thought he was attempting to jest, but he seemed so uncomfortable that she simply said, "Say hello to your mother and daughter for me."

"Oh, that reminds me," he said. "My mother is eager to have you, Miz Matilda, the young lady, and Reverend Russell come to dinner when it's convenient, considering the circumstances with Miz Pansy."

"Thank you," she said.

He plopped the hat on his head and mounted the stallion, which proceeded to kick up the dust along the stretch of path bordered by tall coconut palms.

When Jane returned to the house, Matilda said, "I saw you and Mak talking."

"Yes," she said and smiled. "He mentioned my ring, and we talked about Austin. So Mak MacCauley has nothing to worry about." She flashed a glance at Matilda. "To his way of thinking, where I'm concerned, he's perfectly safe."

Matilda draped her arm around Jane's shoulder and said simply, "Yes, dear."

Chapter 13

Mak wished he hadn't stopped to talk with Jane. He'd simply made a fool of himself. She must take him for a complete idiot. But what could he have done? After she asked to ride the horse, he couldn't very well tell her to climb up and they'd ride together like they had the day she had a problem with her land legs. There had been a reason for it that day. Rather than further embarrass his mom and the reverend and cause more talk than when he'd tried to kill his horse, he'd consented.

But this was another day. She was an engaged woman. He was an avowed single man, and Jane's fiancé likely wouldn't take such an offer from him very kindly. Mak would not have liked for Maylea to climb on a horse with a man she'd just met and trot off. Maybe things were different in Texas.

And he could not let this young woman

get on his horse alone. She still did not know the area. He felt confident he could control Big Brown even under the worst circumstances — that horrible thunderstorm they'd been caught in one time was proof of that, as was the time a wild pig spooked the stallion and Big Brown had reared up unexpectedly.

But no way could Mak chance any woman getting on his stallion alone and riding off. So, his mother said Jane was an equestrienne. But that was under controlled conditions in a confined area with a trained horse, and one she would be accustomed to. That was the kind of riding a lady would do . . . not hightail it off on a horse weighing more than a thousand pounds.

She'd been easy to talk to, fun to talk with. He'd had too many women try and attract his attention. This one did not. She just wanted to ride his horse.

And he could not, would not, allow that.

Perhaps he could show a better side of his character, if there was one, when she came to dinner — if she accepted the invitation.

The following morning, however, when he was less than a mile away from the school, he heard the church bells. That meant one of three things: church would soon begin, but this wasn't Sunday; something wonderful had happened, such as a ship coming in; or something sad had occurred. For death, the bells rang three times and stopped. Then they would ring three more times, and the process would be repeated over and over.

The last time the bells had rung for a dreaded occasion was back in April when Father Damien had died. That remarkable priest had given his life to help the lepers in Molokai. Then he died of leprosy. Word was spread later that he had said the Lord wanted him to spend Easter in heaven.

Father Damien was a remarkable man, willingly sacrificing his young life and health to make seemingly hopeless, outcast human beings a little more comfortable, giving them a glimpse of love and faith.

Now, Mak saw children being led from the school by an adult. When he rode by the church, the elder said, "It's Miss Pansy. She's gone to be with the Lord."

Her role in life was nothing like Father Damien's with the lepers, but it was just as remarkable. Pansy Russell had given her life for the children and adults alike on this Big Island. She'd been known not just as the preacher's wife or as a teacher, but as a servant of the Lord in her own right.

As much as he dreaded it, Mak knew he'd have to see Reverend Russell. Jane let him in and said Matilda and the nurse were putting Pansy's best clothes on her, fixing her hair and face.

Mak extended his hand to Russell. "I'm sorry," was all he could say.

"I know," the reverend said. His sad eyes nevertheless were filled with determination. "Now I know how you feel, Mak." He kept nodding and opened the screen door wider. "Of course there will be no school for the rest of the day."

"No," Mak said, taking a step back. He could not be in the house where a dead woman lay. "I need to let my mother know. She would want that, you know."

"Oh yes. I know. Thanks for stopping by. That means a lot." The reverend's smile held a mixture of sadness and strength.

Mak hadn't been inside a church in three years, not since Maylea's funeral. He only went then because her beautiful body was there in the coffin.

Yes, he believed the words being spoken. Those believing in Jesus were in heaven, were having a better life. He believed that for Maylea, for his dad, for Father Damien, for Pansy Russell.

The reverend spoke comforting words to others, even as the tears streaked his face.

But he'd had Pansy by his side for more than thirty years as they worked together for the Lord. Mak had had Maylea only six short years. He'd been without her for half that time now.

No, on second thought, he was never without her.

And it grieved his heart.

Feeling a light pressure on his hand, he looked down. Leia's small hand lay on his. Her big brown eyes looked up at him. They filled with tears, and her lip trembled. His little girl didn't remember her mother. But she had known Pansy and had loved her. Mak put his arm around her and drew her near.

After the funeral, church members had a meal set out in the fellowship hall. His mother and Leia stayed.

Mak didn't.

He thought of the church that used to mean so much to him. It was where he had given his heart to Jesus as a young lad, where he had later given his heart to Maylea and married her, where he laid her to her final rest.

As foolish as he knew it was, there was no rest for him. He walked out to the graveyard behind the church and down to the stone inscribed MAYLEA MACCAULEY AND

KEIKI, where his wife and child were buried.

Kneeling in the grass, he stared at the stone and the name. He spoke quietly. "Four more months, Maylea. I'll do it for you. It will help. It has to help."

He felt something touch his shoulder. With a slight turn of his head, he saw a hand with a diamond ring on its fourth finger.

"I'm sorry," a soft voice said.

He could only nod.

After a long moment, the hand was gone. He didn't turn. A man couldn't let a woman see him cry.

CHAPTER 14

Pansy was buried on Wednesday, and school resumed the following Monday. After Mak's class, Rev. Russell asked if he could speak with him. They went into the reverend's office. Mak sat across from him at the desk.

"If I could, Mak, I'd like to meet with you and Matilda and Jane to discuss what we might do at the school."

Mak removed his foot from where he'd crossed it over his other knee. He leaned forward. "Maybe we could do that at my home. Mom has wanted to have all of you to dinner. She thought she should . . . wait."

Reverend Russell was already nodding, indicating he understood. "I've been waiting, too, Mak. I've thought about the school and what to do but didn't want to discuss it until after Pansy had gone to be with the Lord. I didn't want to stand in the way in case God wanted to provide a miracle for her." He made a soft sound almost like an ironic laugh. "Or for us, I suppose. She is in her miracle now."

Mak stared at him a moment, having the distinct feeling the reverend was trying to tell him something. But there was really nothing new he could say. Mak knew the facts of life. And the facts of afterlife.

The reverend slapped the arms of his leather chair. "Well Mak, you just tell Rose that we'll be glad to accept that dinner invitation. Any time."

On Friday evening, Mak saw their guests like a silhouette on the horizon. The prancing horse pulled the black surrey against a setting of green grass and clear blue sky.

What would the Buckleys think of his ranch? How would it compare with a wealthy Texan's ranch? Or an oil man's property? He scoffed inwardly, aware that kind of thinking was what turned so many Hawaiians into imitators of western lifestyle many years ago, resulting in their losing much of their own culture.

He walked away from the huge window in the living room, stepped into the foyer, and saw his mother and Leia coming down the curved staircase along the wall. They had probably been watching from an upstairs window.

His mother was dressed elegantly in

western-style clothes that could compete with the finest — clothes that she didn't get to wear too often. Leia was trying to keep her lips still instead of smiling, as if she knew how beautiful she looked in her yellow dress trimmed with ruffles and a huge green sash. Her black hair curled naturally but now lay in ringlets and was adorned on one side with a pink, yellow-centered flower.

"My two beautiful girls," he said. His mother smiled broadly. She knew she was a handsome woman. Leia laughed delightedly. She made a small curtsy. "Thank you, Daddy."

All right. She was already practicing her manners.

"I'll go out and greet them, Mother," he said.

"Good," she said. She usually greeted their guests. Depending upon who they were, sometimes the housekeeper invited guests in. Feeling quite well-attired himself, in his western-style suit, Mak wished to give the impression he was not always a grump nor a crybaby. He was the man of this . . . this . . . ranch and this house.

He went out and stood on the porch as the reverend's surrey meandered up the long, stone driveway.

"Aloha, Reverend." They shook hands.

Mak held out his hand to the woman who looked as fiery as an evening sunset that lit up the world in bright red. She wore a red satin dress with the cut of the bodice like something the missionaries would have banned a few decades back. Decorating her chest was a strand of rubies set in silver. Her hair was a deeper red and in a high updo of curls and rolls and jeweled combs. She could pass for a Hawaiian landscape at sunset.

"Aloha and komo mai."

"Thank you," she said, setting her pointy-toed shoes on the ground and moving aside.

"Miz Buckley," he said to the next pair of pointy shoes. He lifted his hands and his gaze and was astounded by the contrast between the woman he'd just helped from the surrey and this one.

"Aloha and komo mai."

She lay her gloved hand in his and stepped down. "Aloha and komo mai to you, too."

Leia giggled and put her hand over her mouth.

Jane huffed. "What did I do wrong this time?"

"I'm sure you know *aloha* by now," Mak said. "*Komo mai* means welcome."

She and the others laughed lightly. "Thanks for the lesson. I do want to learn

Hawaiian."

"I can teach you some words," Leia said. "And you can teach me some words. I want to learn about that filthy . . ." She looked up at his mother. "What was that?"

"Never mind, dear."

The way the two Miz Buckleys shared a quick glance, Mak thought they probably guessed what kind of conversation Leia might have been privy to.

"We've known each other long enough not to be so formal," Jane said. He realized he had been thinking of her as Jane all along. "I'm just plain Jane." She smiled. "By the way, you're looking mighty fine this evening."

He wondered if that should have been his line, but he hadn't wanted to be overly complimentary to any of them. He felt, along with Shakespeare, that discretion was the better part of valor. And he didn't have to mistake her remark as flirting, because she was an engaged woman.

He nodded, smiled, and observed that she was anything but plain. She was as refreshingly beautiful as her aunt was fiery beautiful. The high neck trimmed in a soft ruffle was light blue, and her eyes had turned that same color. Yes, they must be hazel. They'd been gray that first day when she'd thrown up, then green at the Ti leaves, now blue. Little swirls of golden brown hair lay across her forehead and along the sides of her face. The rest of her hair was arranged in a thick roll.

Until the fiery Buckley woman said, "Just a moment, Pilar. Mr. MacCauley will help you down," he'd forgotten there was a third person to exit the surrey.

He quickly held out his hand to the young girl, who looked about ready to jump out and could have done so easily. This, however, was the polite way. She looked pretty in an elegant dress, and her hair was pulled back from her face. As she stepped down, he saw a white bow fastened at the back of her hair.

He nodded at the stable boy who waited at the side of the house, then heard the women greeting each other and passing around compliments on their clothes and looks. Reverend Russell caught his arm, leaned close, and said, "These beautiful women are our dinner partners. How lucky can a man get?"

"Indeed," Mak said and laughed lightly. He walked ahead, held the screen door open, and bowed slightly as he gestured for them to enter.

In the foyer, they stopped as Matilda commented on the beauty of the white, two-story frame house and the elegance of the foyer and staircase.

"Thank you," his mother said. "I'm sure it doesn't compare with your plantation home in Texas." She gave Jane a knowing look. "I've seen some of that kind."

"Maybe not as big as . . . my daddy's," Jane said, placing the emphasis on *my daddy's,* implying it wasn't hers. "But it's just as beautiful. In Texas, they just have to make everything bigger."

She cast a teasing glance at Mak when she said, "Even the stars are bigger." He could feel his cheeks color slightly, but he smiled. "Before we go in," she said, "I have something for Leia."

Leia stepped up to her, her dark eyes shining and looked expectantly while Jane opened a shiny blue bag and took out a smaller white satin bag drawn closed with a drawstring. "Just put your fingers in the top and pull it apart."

While Leia did that, Jane said, "This is my own special lei that I'd like to give you."

"Ohhh." Leia's little mouth made an *O,* and Mak knew she was truly pleased with the strand of small pearls.

"I know it's not as big or as colorful as the lei you gave me, but this is a lei from

Texas. They're pearls."

"Can I wear it?"

"Here, let me," Rose said and fastened the string of pearls around Leia's neck. Leia touched them, looked down, and then held out her arms as she rushed to Jane and threw her arms around her waist.

"I looove this," she said, after stepping back. "I never had any pearls before."

"I'm glad you like it," Jane said, and then his mother offered to show them through the house.

Mak tried not to let his thoughts show on his face, but everything reminded him of his loss. Leia's loss. Leia should have a mother who gave her pearls, who fastened them around her neck. He should have a wife to show guests the house.

He was beginning to think it was a mistake to have a woman around, even if she did belong to someone else.

Nevermore pecked at his brain like Edgar Allan Poe's raven. And although he had his land legs, he felt a stir of accustomed nausea.

CHAPTER 15

Jane loved the house. She learned that the ranch and house had been left to Mak by his father, wanting to make sure Rose would be taken care of. It was about half the size of her daddy's plantation house, and Rose's comment confirmed that when she said, "There are four bedrooms upstairs and a sitting room that doubles as a playroom and a schoolroom for Leia."

"Could Miss Jane see it?" Leia said. "I want her to know how much I've learned since she might be my teacher."

Jane didn't intend to be a schoolteacher and wasn't sure what to say, so she remained silent, but she smiled at Leia. Her uncle Russell came to her rescue. "Leia, we don't know yet who will be teaching the classes. Your dad is doing a wonderful job."

Mak lifted his hands as if to ward off such a thought. He emitted a short laugh. "I'm a rancher, Russ, not a teacher. Anytime one of these ladies wants the job, I'm fine with it."

"I do want to discuss that." He put his arm around Matilda. "Even if she is my sister, I can truthfully say this fine lady would work her fingers to the bone to help somebody else."

Matilda's scoff of distress made him lean away from her, but the affectionate look in his eyes was evident. "But I know, too, she'd like to explore this island from the white sands to the black sands as soon as I can assure her I'm all right without her telling me what to do."

Matilda scoffed. "I took a five-month-long trip for this? That's a brother for you. Wait till I tell you how he used to treat me."

"Now Tildy," he said. "You were the more spirited of us children. You don't want me telling stories on you, do you?"

She gave him a warning stare. "Let's change the subject right now."

Rose spoke up. "Russell, you didn't mention the green sand beaches."

"Green sand?" Matilda's mouth remained open until she found words again. "Are you serious?"

Before Rose could answer, Leia was nodding. "It's really green sand. Grandmother and her friend took me there."

Mak said, "If we're ever going to have our dinner, maybe we'd better get this tour over with."

"I believe our next room is the dining room," Rose said. They followed her down the hallway, past the kitchen on the right, and entered the spacious dining room. Over the table hung a crystal chandelier, holding many candles.

When Jane glanced down she noticed Mak looking at her. Did he suspect, or know, that Texas had electricity already?

Along two walls, the sunlight shone through wide windows that offered a view of green lawn and lush foliage, a lovely contrast to the elegant dining room.

Mak had her uncle Russell sit at one end of the long table while he sat at the other.

"Sit across from me," Rose said to Matilda, and they took their places at each side of Mak. Jane sat beside Matilda and Pilar next to Jane. Leia sat across from them, beside Rose.

After her uncle asked the blessing on the food, a heavyset, gray-haired, woman who looked to be maybe in her sixties, entered the room with a huge silver platter. "This is Coco," Rose said. "She and her husband had a restaurant in Hilo for many years. Now, we're fortunate to have her with us.

She's the best cook in all of Hawaii."

Coco seemed stiff and unfriendly. "Aloha," she said in a monotone voice. "I've prepared a special dish for you. Broiled crocodile eyes on a bed of Ki leaves, smothered in coconut juice."

Jane didn't know what the others were doing, but she opted to look at Leia, hoping a child's expression might tell her this could not be dinner. Leia's lips were pressed together, and her little eyebrows lifted slightly and her widened eyes simply moved from one side to the other as if this were an everyday dinner item. But Jane thought the little girl seemed to be trying a little too hard to act like everything was normal.

In complete silence, Coco walked over to the table, set down the silver platter, and lifted the lid, revealing the most delectable piece of what looked and smelled like beef with something else beside it.

Coco's face relaxed, and Jane felt sure they all breathed easier. "I serve the beef in case anyone doesn't like fish. This is a prize Hawaiian fish called *opakapuka.*" She asked them to take their forks and sample the fish.

Jane wasn't sure about the *puka* sound of the fish, and gingerly placed a bite in her mouth. "Wonderful," she said, not caring if much of it still lay on her tongue. "I've never tasted fish so good." She looked around at the others, and they were nodding. Mak was smiling.

"I'll be back," Coco said.

"May I help?" Pilar said.

Nobody seemed to know what to say for a long moment. "Oh," Matilda said. "Pilar is a cook, too. I know she'd love to see the kitchen."

"That would be very nice," Rose said.

"Me, too?" Leia asked.

Rose nodded. "That would be nice, too."

At that moment, the dinner became very informal. Coco was even more congenial as she explained that taro was a kind of yam. Pilar brought in dishes of fresh vegetables of every conceivable kind, and Leia brought the cold food.

Coco dished out a small, stuffed green leaf and laid it on each plate. "This is rice in taro leaves," she said proudly. "You can put those around at each place," she said to Leia, who brought in two dessert dishes, then went back for more.

"This is Hawaii's famous *haupia* pudding made from coconuts. And be sure to try the mountain apple jam on your bread."

"This is fabulous," Matilda said. "I've traveled many places in the world, and your Coco has outdone them all." She looked at

Pilar. "Most all of them, anyway."

Pilar smiled. "Probably all."

Jane knew Pilar had just eliminated her mother as the world's best cook.

Uncle Russell was nodding and chewing, plowing into the food.

"You really are eating some of the best food Hawaii has to offer," Rose said. "There are many restaurants here, a lot of Japanese, Chinese, and Portuguese in particular, and their food is good. But this is a collection favored by most people."

"You did give me a scare, Coco," Matilda said. "I don't think I'm ready for crocodile eyes."

Coco stood with her hands folded in front of her while they sampled the various kinds of food.

"She does something like that every time we have guests," Rose said. "That's why they say they aren't going to accept a dinner invitation unless Coco is the cook."

The older woman had transformed from a person of sternness into someone who seemed much like a member of the family. Her laughter, smile, and shining brown eyes made her look ten years younger than when she'd come into the dining room.

"She was like that in the restaurant," Mak said. "That's one reason it was the most

116

popular place to eat in the area."

The woman's body seemed to laugh with her. "When people come from other countries to the island, they should sample good, real Hawaiian food. I'll be back." She walked to the doorway and looked over her shoulder. "And I do hide in the hallway and listen to conversations."

"I like that woman," Matilda said.

"Oh we love her," Rose said. "She's so dear to us. Our guests always say they'd love for her to join us at dinners, but she won't. Says she has her place."

"That reminds me of my mother," Pilar said. "She's a cook for the Buckleys. Oh," she added quickly, "my mother doesn't joke like that. She just cooks."

Jane felt the others now realized that's why Pilar wanted to help. Matilda spoke up. "Your mother has a particularly difficult time, Pilar."

She nodded. "If she were here, she wouldn't let me sit at this table. She's afraid I'll get big ideas."

"Well, like I've said before," Matilda said, "we're in Hawaii now. Let your ideas be . . ." She lifted her hands in the air and wiggled her fingers. "Let them be . . . flowers and sunshine and palm trees."

Soon the conversation was dominated by

Matilda and Rose exchanging stories about their travels.

Jane halfway listened but was delighting in the delicious food served by a cook who had pretended to be stern. Was some of Mak's aloofness a pretense, too? Or did he really think no woman could break through his carefully guarded defenses?

CHAPTER 16

It seemed nobody wanted to move. "I am completely stuffed," Jane said.

"Me, too," Leia said, as Coco came in with a silver pot. "But I have room for coffee."

"Sure," Mak said. "In about ten years."

She grinned and picked up her milk glass.

"This is Kona coffee," Coco said, pouring them each a cup. "The world's best."

Uncle Russell had already introduced Kona coffee to Jane and Matilda, who were nodding as Mak affirmed Coco's statement. "That's no exaggeration," he said. "It's in great demand throughout the rest of the world. It's one of Hawaii's greatest exports."

"I will bring cream," Coco said.

Jane sipped the black coffee. "Delicious," she said. "But I do take cream."

While waiting, she glanced at Mak. "You call the ranch *Bele Chere*?" They'd ridden under the sign at the top of a wrought iron entry. "That sounds French."

"You know French, then?"

"I studied it in college."

"So, what does it mean in French?"

"Let her guess, Daddy." Leia had such expectation in her eyes that Jane figured she was waiting for her to say something funny again. She probably would.

"Mmm. *Bele* is close to *belle,* meaning beautiful. *Chere.* I don't know. Sounds like it would be close to *cherie,* meaning friend. So *Bele Chere* means *good friend,* or *beautiful friend.*"

After she tried to guess, Leia said, *"Bele Chere* means *beautiful loving."*

"Living," Mak corrected, as they all laughed lightly. *"Beautiful living.* In the olden days, it meant something like that, could be *good life, beautiful life.* My dad named the ranch. It's Scottish."

"What does Leia mean?" Jane asked.

"Meadow," Mak said, the look in his eyes as soft as his voice.

"Grandmother says I'm like a meadow full of pretty flowers."

Jane smiled. "I think she's right."

Leia nodded. "I do, too."

They all laughed. Ah, the beauty of innocent youth.

When Coco returned with cream, Jane

stirred it into her coffee. She smiled and looked across at Leia. "Leia, your beautiful skin is the color of Kona coffee with a touch of cream in it. Very beautiful."

"*Mahalo*. That means *thank you*." She looked at Jane for a moment. "Yours has little speckles on it. On your nose across here."

"Yes, it does," Jane said.

Leia squinted as she stared. "It's a little like ants crawling on the white sand."

Matilda was the only one who dared to laugh, and she did it vigorously.

"Did you put them on there, or did they just grow that way?" She was very serious.

"They just grew."

Leia looked wistful. "I wish I had some. I like them."

Jane nodded. "Mahalo. I do, too." She smiled at the little girl, giving her so much attention. "But I didn't always like them. They've faded through the years, but I took a lot of teasing when I was young."

"Me, too," Leia said, her expression sympathetic.

Mak spoke up. "What do you mean, Leia? Who's teasing you?"

Her lips formed an *O* and her eyes closed. "Sorry. Grandmother told me to forget it. I guess I forgot to forget it."

Rose appeared uncomfortable under Mak's stare. She waved a hand as if dismissing it. "Oh you know, Mak. That was last year when a man came to get the horse you'd trained, and his little boy said unkind things to her."

Leia was nodding. "He said I was crippled and ugly."

Jane joined Matilda and Pilar, who made protesting noises, and Jane said, "You're beautiful, Leia."

Leia nodded. "Now I am, but not when my leg gets tired."

Pilar was young enough to ask the question that Jane had on her mind and figured Matilda did, too. "Why does your leg get tired?"

Leia's face made movements like she was trying to think. "I forgot." But she smiled then. "But my limp is fading," she said, "like Miss Jane's freckles."

The tension was thick as that chunk of beef, Jane thought.

"What I want to know," Matilda said, setting down her coffee cup. "Is about the hula. I hear it mentioned often, but it's said like a Baptist talking about whiskey. Makes the upper lip curl up. Is this not polite dinner conversation?" She looked toward Leia.

"Or not to be discussed in mixed company?"

"No, it's fine," Rose assured her, seeming relieved that the subject of Leia's leg had changed to something else, but Mak's face still looked cloudy. "The hula is a kind of dance the early Hawaiians did. After missionaries came, it was forbidden. The people were taught that God would not accept them unless they wore clothes and stopped doing the hula."

"The missionaries were mistaken," Uncle Russell said. "They thought the hula was connected with nudity. In the last few years, we've come to understand that the hula was the Hawaiians' way of communicating about their culture. Before the missionaries came, they had no written language, so they acted out their stories."

"That's right," Mak added. "The gentle swaying of their bodies and hand movements are like sign language. It's a natural artistic form of the spoken word. We point, we clap, hit, strike our fist against the palm of the other hand, slap the table, shake hands, move the hand as a warning." As if proving his point he looked at the position of his upraised hands. "We gesture."

"And this," Leia said, smacking her left hand with her right one.

"Now Leia," Rose said, "How many times have I spanked your hand?"

Mak spoke up. "Mother, if I remember correctly, once was enough." He slapped the side of his thigh. "And that was back here."

Leia's dark eyes were filled with love as she looked at her dad, smiling and nodding. "But she won't spank me there because it might hurt my leg."

"But speaking of the hula," Rose said as if in a hurry to change the subject again. "The king had a birthday party. My husband and I attended. I believe that was about fifteen years ago. Anyway, that party lasted for two weeks. Two thousand people were invited, and he brought back the hula. That helped make it more acceptable."

"And you danced the hula?" Matilda asked.

"Well . . ." The lovely woman touched the side of her coiffure and spoke in a rather sultry voice. "The party lasted for two weeks. He was the king. What's one to do?"

They all laughed.

Rose seemingly changed the subject when she said, "I'm sure you have electricity in Texas."

"Recently," Jane said. "In the big cities."

"We don't yet," Rose said, then returned

to the subject of the king. "But a couple of years ago, the king installed a fantastic electric system at the palace. That cost more than it did to build the palace."

"Does the king —" Jane and Matilda both started to ask the question at the same time. Jane motioned to Matilda, who finished the question. "Does he still have his parties?" Jane knew the two of them would love an invitation to the palace.

"He does occasionally," Rose said. "He always throws a party before the island's most important horse race."

Jane would have liked to hear more about that, but Leia spoke up. "Come to my party."

"Oh, you're having a party?"

She nodded. "I have one every year of my life for my birthday."

Jane smiled at her. "How old will you be?"

She held up six fingers.

"Six. That's a good age."

Leia smiled and nodded, causing her dark curls to bounce against her face and shoulders. Such a pretty little girl. Her mother must have been beautiful. Well, her dad wasn't exactly a hobgoblin, but they'd said Leia looked like her mother.

Seeing that they had finished their coffee, Rose made a suggestion. "Mak, Jane might enjoy seeing the horses, since she's an expert horsewoman."

"I'm not expert," Jane rebutted, feeling the twinge of being second best.

"Oh, Matilda says you are."

"Matilda embellishes."

They all laughed, including Matilda, as if they agreed.

The idea of seeing the horses excited Jane. "I would love to see them. And I need to find out if there's a place where I could rent a horse for my own transportation. Matilda, would you like to see the horses?"

Matilda waved a hand. "Oh honey, I've seen enough back ends of horses to last me a lifetime. Rose has offered to show me the upstairs and some of those comfortable-looking dresses so many women wear for everyday."

Rose smiled at her. "Yes, and I want to hear more about your travels. And Texas."

"Jane and Pilar heard my stories over and over on the voyage. I think they'd get seasick hearing them again."

"Miss Jane," Mak said, seeming sincere instead of sullen, "I'd be happy to show you the horses. Some of them, anyway."

"Well, this being a ranch, I wouldn't expect to see them all. So I accept, if you don't mind leaving your company."

"You are my company. And there's something I'd like to ask you." He congenially looked at her uncle. "Russ, I know you've seen them before, but would you like to join us at the stables?"

"What I'd like to do," her uncle said, "is talk Coco out of another piece of bread smeared with mountain apple jam and a cup of coffee, sit on the front porch in that rocking chair, and just eat, drink, and . . . sit." He chuckled. "Maybe prepare a sermon on gluttony."

"Leia," Rose said, "why don't you show Pilar your rooms and collections? She might like to see your schoolroom. If Miss Jane doesn't teach, Reverend Russell has said Miss Matilda has some good things she could teach us all."

"Oh," Leia said, "I would like Miss Jane to be my teacher." She pointed to Matilda. "And you, if you can sit still long enough."

Matilda smiled. "I'll keep that in mind."

Leia reached for Pilar's hand. "Do you have Little People and Night Marchers in Texas?"

Pilar shrugged a shoulder. "No."

Leia led Pilar away. "I can tell you about them. You need to know, to be safe."

Just as Jane was about to ask, Rose sighed. "Children and their imaginations. Okay you two, go on," she said to Jane and Mak. "Matilda and I have fashion and travel to discuss."

If she didn't know better, and if they all didn't know she was engaged to be married, Jane might think somebody was trying to set her up with Mak MacCauley.

CHAPTER 17

"Mark," Jane said as they walked across the velvety green lawn. "What, or who, are the Little People Leia mentioned?"

He looked down at her and exclaimed, "Amazing." Then he laughed. "I mean your eyes. They've become as green as a Ti leaf."

Her chin lifted. "You mean like cooked and stuffed with rice?"

"Hardly."

She liked his laugh. She thought it was amazing how cordial he could be as long as she wasn't asking to ride his horse. "My eyes do that," she said. "They'll turn dull again in another setting."

He seemed about to say something but closed his mouth. He opened it again and said, "Mine are always a dull brown."

She might have said she thought his eyes quite dark and mysterious and she'd like to know what he seemed to carefully conceal behind them, but he quickly said,

"This way."

They'd come to the lush foliage at the end of the lawn, and he led her down a shaded path bordered by Ti and other bushes and trees she didn't know the names of.

"About the Little People," he said. "I think most cultures have their fairy tales. Or tall tales. Like most legends, stories are based on fact. It's believed the Menehunes were a race of people living here long ago. People of other places came in and conquered them. The conquered people were considered inferior, and the word *Menehune* came to mean *commoner.*"

"Like the Romans and Jews," Jane said. "The conquerors always think the conquered are inferior." At his quick glance, her thoughts came closer to the present. "Or like Indians, Mexicans, and . . . slavery." She drew in a breath. "Are the natural Hawaiians looked upon that way?"

"There's a parallel," he said. "As you mentioned, it's in all cultures. Sometimes it's called class distinction, society, caste system. But before we get too morbid, let me add that through the centuries, the Menehunes have become legend as Little People, no more than three feet high. They do good deeds. If sharks are about to attack you, the Little People can come in their little tiny canoes and beat them away with their paddles. You never see them. They do their good deeds at night and are responsible for many blessings."

"I can see that children might enjoy the stories," Jane said. "But Christians wouldn't believe the stories, would they?"

"I don't know," he said as they walked from the foliage into what seemed to be an entirely different world. Stretched out before her was an elaborate stable bordered by a corral.

As they neared the stables, Jane stopped in her tracks, forgetting anything but what came into view ahead of her.

"How magnificent." She hurried to the fence, heading for the huge black stallion glistening like velvet in the soft evening sun. A rider dismounted and held the reins.

"Careful," Mak said. "That's Panai, my racehorse."

Jane saw the big black eyes sizing her up. He snorted, as if trying to scare her away. Jane laughed but kept her distance. "Why, you big pretender. You don't scare me at all. You're all huffs and snorts."

Like your owner, crossed her mind.

"Don't be too sure," Mak said. "Miss Jane, meet my jockey, Chico Garcia."

Chico was a small, middle-aged man who

looked as dark as some of the Mexicans in Texas. His intelligent eyes were as black as Panai's.

Chico held the reins. "Stay there," Chico said to Panai and stood between Jane and the horse.

"Aloha Miss," Chico said. Creases formed in his weathered face when he smiled.

Jane kept pretending she was paying no attention to Panai, but she knew he was watching. A proud horse, waiting for her praise of him.

"This is Panai. Panai, Miss Jane."

Jane started to take a step, but Mak said, "No, don't approach him. Chico, take him inside."

"See you later, Panai," Jane said.

She smelled the welcome aroma of horse-flesh and hay. The horse had a large stall, more like an apartment.

In the stall, Panai turned and stood at the half door. Jane saw other horses with their heads sticking over their half-doors, turned their way. "I think the other horses are in awe of Panai," she said, noting that Panai looked at her when she said his name.

"No," Mak said. "They've seen him for many years. They must be in awe of you."

"I —" She started to deny that but became still. Panai moved forward and stood as if not seeing her.

Jane stepped closer.

"Careful," Mak warned. "He has teeth."

Jane studied that huge, magnificent, black velvet head with the white mark of a champion blatantly displayed down the front of his face.

She brought her hand up to stroke his head. His big black eyes held what? Curiosity? She spoke softly to him and patted his neck. His head moved up and down.

"You have a way, Miss," Chico said. "He never lets anybody do that but me and Mister Mak."

"He knows I love him," Jane said, "not just appreciate his beauty and strength. I love him because he's . . . a horse. A wonderful animal."

Chico stayed near and held the reins. "He tolerates males but shies away from females."

"Well," she said. "Maybe he's decided it's time for a little female companionship, a female friend."

Jane dared not look at Mak. She sensed the silence. The horse and his owner were somewhat alike. No females — threatening ones, that is.

As if in answer, Mak said, "We don't want him going soft. He has a goal. The three of us have a goal."

Jane looked at him. "To stay away from females?"

Even Mak laughed good-naturedly along with Chico. "Seems I've been talked about behind my back. I mean, our goal is to win a race. And Chico needs to take care of the horse."

Chico said, "He likes you."

For a moment their eyes met. For an instant she thought, *Who? Panai or Mak?* Then Chico said, "Almost as much as he likes an apple or carrot treat."

Well, that settled that — she hoped.

After a final pat to Panai's neck, Jane walked down the passageways to the other stalls, adequate but smaller than Panai's.

"These are for the carriages and daily riding," Mak explained. She spoke to a couple of stable boys grooming the horses, probably having recently been brought in from the range. Each of the horses was eager for a pat or a rub.

"Which do you like best?" Mak asked.

"I like them all, but —"

"Other than Panai," Mak said. "He's not in the same category."

Jane nodded. Panai was special, set apart. Like some people seemed to be born for a special purpose or with extraordinary abilities.

"Okay, let me see. Oh, this one I know. Hey, I think I've ridden on you." She rubbed his face.

Mak patted his neck. "Big Brown," he said.

"Sure is. What's his name?"

"Big Brown."

Jane laughed lightly. "Oh, he likes me very much. See, he's trying to nuzzle me."

Mak allowed it. "Something Panai would never do."

Jane swept her gaze down to Panai, thinking, *You heard that, didn't you, Panai? But we'll see. We'll see.*

"These two," Mak said, walking farther past the stalls, "are ready to be ridden by others. Which would you choose for yourself?"

Jane looked them over. One was solid brown and looked to have a good nature. The white one was a wee bit smaller but shook its head, and she suspected it had a frisky nature and thought they'd love to ride over the range together. They seemed equally receptive to her. She felt their necks, their shoulders, gently rubbed their faces.

"I can't decide," she said. "Which would you choose for me?"

"I'll think on it," he said.

They walked back up the passageway. Chico was brushing Panai's hips.

"Nice meeting you, Chico. Panai." She winked.

She could have sworn the horse winked back. At least she knew he blinked, which upon first encounter he had not done. A horse could learn very difficult tricks. Winking was probably the least difficult.

Upon entering the stables, she hadn't noticed much of anything except the big horse as they turned left. Now on the right, she saw the carriages, the surreys, a good supply of vehicles.

"These are mighty fine," she said, touching first one, then another of the handsome vehicles, including a hansom, a landau, and a surrey, in which several people could ride in style.

"Now, what I wanted to ask you."

Jane faced him with an expectant feeling. Since he considered her no personal threat, would he offer to let her ride with him over the range?

CHAPTER 18

"I was wondering," Mak said, "Do you think you and Matilda and Pilar would like a ride over the ranch?"

"Oh my, yes."

"In this?" He tapped the wooden side of a wagon with his forefinger.

He watched her touch the wooden sides that were about two feet high, then look into the wagon in which eight people could be seated comfortably.

"Is this a farm wagon?"

"Yes." He wondered what kind of vehicles seven people would take for an outing in Texas. Of course, that would depend upon how they were dressed. Jane and their other guests were dressed for a semiformal dinner. "Or we could take a couple of surreys."

"No, the wagon's perfect," she said, and he believed she meant it, until she added, "If it's not clean, we could sit on a bandana." A trace of mischief was in her eyes.

At that, a stable boy appeared from the passageway. "I cleaned it, Mr. Mak."

"I was kidding about the bandana," she said. "Do I need to return it to you?"

He reared back and stuck out his hands. "Oh please don't. I never want to see that again."

"I can hook up the fillies, Mr. Mak."

Mak nodded, aware that the stable boy — and Chico, too — probably strained to hear every word they spoke. Other than his mother, Jane was the only woman who had been in this carriage house and stable since Maylea. But they would see her ring, or he could tell them before anyone started rumors about anything possibly being personal.

"I think they'd love riding in this and seeing the ranch. I know I will."

"It's not too . . . rustic?"

"It's perfect."

Mak smiled and nodded to the stable boy, who struck off down the passageway toward the horses.

Mak asked the reverend to sit up front with him and have the ladies ride in the seats behind them.

Listening to the women talk and his mother describe certain sections, Mak felt he was really seeing his own ranch for the

138

first time in a long time.

He allowed the two dapple grays to trot-walk along acres and acres of green rolling fields, past grazing sheep and cattle. At one point, they stopped to watch a herd of wild mustangs disappear along the slope of a distant mountain.

He heard his mother explaining about the bunkhouses, the many corrals, the small houses where some of the paniolos lived.

Beyond that was endless acres of green merging with white wavy lines of tide rushing in and out from a royal blue sea that melted into a lighter blue sky dotted with a few wispy clouds.

"My property ends here," Mak explained, pointing to a fence. "That's the beginning of a sugar plantation. All that is sugar cane. Belongs to friends of mine, the Honeycutts."

"Honeycutts?" Pilar said. "That must be where Susanne Honeycutt invited me to go on Sunday."

"I'm going, too," Leia said.

Mak heard his mother explain, "Leia's grandparents on her mother's side live at the plantation. But, Pilar, you must know Susanne from school."

"Yes, we're both seniors."

"Well, Rose," Matilda said. "Since our

young girls will be away, why don't you visit with me on Sunday?"

"That would be perfect," Rose said. "I'll be at church."

They'd been gone for about thirty minutes. "I'll take you back around a different way," Mak told them.

"I could go on forever," Jane said. "This is the most beautiful countryside I've ever seen."

"We do still have a ride back to town, you know," Russell reminded them.

"Okay," Jane said. "But if we're going to head back, there's something I have to do." Mak stopped the horses when she began climbing over the seats.

"Uncle Russell, change places with me, will you?"

They managed to make the exchange, but Mak wasn't about to sit anywhere but right beside her. He should have expected it when she reached over and clutched the reins. "It's either this, or you walk home."

He handed over the reins.

After a while, he quit watching her every move and even enjoyed the ride when she had the horses canter. When she had them come close to a gallop, he murmured, "Ump uh," and she slowed them.

He could not remember when someone

else had given him a ride. He was always at the reins. All he needed to do was occasionally tell her the way to go until, in the far distance, his home rose like a man's castle atop the gentle slope.

Seeing it as he thought his visitors would, he wondered how long it had been since he appreciated what he had.

When they returned to the house, Jane let her passengers out at the house. She drove him down to the stables. Chico smiled broadly, as did the stable boy, who came to take the wagon inside and unhitch the grays.

"Not bad," Mak said, "for a lady."

She gave him a reprimanding glance but again thanked him profusely.

She walked down to Panai, and again the horse let her touch him. Chico was right: She had a way with horses, Mak realized. They took to her, trusted her, and she wasn't afraid. She'd handled the grays expertly. "You asked about rentals," he said.

"Yes," she said, keeping her eyes on Panai, apparently sensing he was sizing her up, too. "I want to have my own transportation."

There were rental places in town, but one couldn't always be sure what one might get. He leaned against the stall near Panai. "It looks like our families have plans for Sunday. If you're available after church, I could bring a horse for you."

Her eyes, now duller than vivid green or blue but filled with anticipation, stared into his own. "You've decided which one?"

He smiled. "I'll surprise you."

He'd already surprised her by being so cordial. Was it only because she was a guest at his home? Or because she wore an engagement ring? Maybe some woman should teach him a lesson, that he was just as susceptible to a woman's charms as any other man.

Not more than ten minutes later, Jane thought she should be horsewhipped. The big question in her mind should not be what kind of man was Mak MacCauley, but what kind of woman was Jane Buckley.

CHAPTER 19

Almost as soon as they were settled in the surrey, they waved good-bye again, and Uncle Russell drove them down the stone drive, Matilda spoke up in a concerned way. "What a bad time that child has had in such a short while. Losing her mother and having surgery on her leg."

Pilar was sympathetic. "I asked Leia, and she said she doesn't remember her leg getting hurt. She just knows she fell and twisted her knee and the doctors had to operate."

"Rose told me," Matilda said, "that Leia was on the horse with Maylea. As Maylea fell, she held onto Leia, protecting her the best she could, but Leia's leg was twisted under her. Children's bones are hard to break," she said. "It's the twisting that was harder to deal with than if there had been a clean break."

Uncle Russell looked over his shoulder at

them. "That was such a bad, bad time for Mak and Rose, but hardest for Mak. Rose had been through enough to know to turn to the Lord and others for comfort. Mak turned against God and became aloof from most others. For a while, they didn't know if Leia's leg would continue to grow the way it should."

"Jane, did Mak talk to you about it?" Matilda said, her expression troubled.

"No," Jane said.

"Like I said," Russell tossed back, "he doesn't open up to anyone about it."

Jane felt like the dirt along the road they traveled and thought she deserved to be run over by the wheels of the surrey. She hadn't had enough decency to remember to ask Mak about Leia's leg.

She felt Matilda's light pat on her hand, looked at it, and then smiled faintly at her aunt. Matilda must have thought the moisture in Jane's eyes was about Leia's plight. In a way, it was. But in another way, it was about her own plight. In the stables, she'd been thinking about horses and even entertained the idea of being able to appeal to Mak MacCauley.

What kind of hopeless creature was she?

Her other hand covered Matilda's for a moment. Matilda loved her. But Matilda

144

didn't know how thoughtless she could be.

Did she?

If Uncle Russell preached about sins of omission, she'd probably shrivel up and sink into a hole somewhere.

Sunday morning at church, Rose said Mak had taken Leia to her grandparents earlier. Pilar left with the Honeycutts. Rose, Matilda, and Uncle Russ rode into town to have lunch at a restaurant.

Jane ate a banana, changed into her riding clothes, and waited outside for Mak. "Why this one?" she said when he showed up with Cinnamon.

"After considering the pros and cons," he said with a trace of humor, "it came down to color. Since you have chameleon eyes, I didn't want to chance them turning white."

He did have a quirky sense of humor. "So you want to see my eyes turn rusty-colored?"

"Look." He rubbed his hand along the horse's side. "She's the color of your hair in the sun. A golden brown." He gestured. "Shall we?"

She exhaled heavily. "I'm more than ready."

"Fine. Since your first experience of riding on the beach a few weeks ago left a lot to be desired, I thought we might trot along a stretch of beach that's about three miles long. How's that?"

Sitting astride the horse she huffed. "Trot?"

"Yes." His determined tone left no doubt he meant it. "You and the horse need to get to know each other. Isn't that what you would tell a child you were teaching to ride?"

This was a test she surmised. If she didn't behave, he wouldn't allow her to teach Leia. And every little girl should learn to ride properly. Her expression must have been one of acquiescence because he pulled on the reins to turn Big Brown, and they trotted off together.

As they rode through town, Jane looked at the restaurant windows. "Rose and Matilda are probably in one of those places having lunch."

He looked over. "Mother really enjoys Matilda's company." He laughed. "But who doesn't?"

Jane smiled at that. Matilda had a way of making everyone feel comfortable. As they rode out of town, she said what she'd planned to say for the past two days. "I wanted to ask about Leia's leg. Does that have something to do with her not having learned to ride?"

"Partly," he said, a furrow appearing between his brows. "Of course, she couldn't for a long time after the surgery, and she didn't want to be near a horse. Later, she seemed to have forgotten what happened, but she still has a fear. She wants to ride, begs me, but when I start to put her on a horse, that fear sets in. Then my apprehension surfaces, and horses sense that. She's determined, in spite of the fear." He took a deep breath and looked out over Big Brown's head. "But so was Maylea."

Jane closed her eyes against what he must be feeling.

"The doctors say the leg is healed, but the right one is weaker than the left. As she grows, she will probably experience pain. Exercise should help the leg grow stronger. Horseback riding probably would."

Jane knew horses picked up on a rider's emotions. Maybe she could help Leia overcome her fear. Mak's was a fear of a different kind. Could anyone help him overcome his?

"In Texas, do you train your horses in the ocean?" he asked when they reached the beach.

"The horses I have for my classes have already been trained. I just need to train the child and horse to accept each other and teach the child how to get the horse to know and obey commands or movements."

"Here," he said, "a wild mustang or a belligerent horse receives a lot of his training in the ocean."

She wouldn't mind getting into the ocean in a bathing outfit, but in her riding clothes? "Is that what we're going to do?"

"Yes. Let's trot on down."

If he hadn't hesitated before saying that, she might have believed him. She shook her head, and he smiled.

"Okay Mak. So I asked a stupid question. This might be another one. Why do you train them in the ocean?"

"Not stupid at all. We take them into the ocean because they can't buck or kick while getting used to a rider and commands. That tames them. And too, it's not a bad idea for a horse to learn how to swim."

"Makes sense," she said. She soon found herself enjoying the Sunday afternoon trot along a white sand beach with a clear blue sky overhead. A deep blue ocean stretched alongside the beach, its waves caressing the shore, reminiscent of the breeze causing the palm leaves to sway. She could understand how the early Hawaiians, who had no written language, would express themselves with swaying bodies and moving hands.

This was a perfect day. Come to think of it, she couldn't think of a day in Hawaii that hadn't been perfect. And Uncle Russell said he did not want anyone catering to him but for them to enjoy Hawaii. He was delighted when she told him that Mak was bringing a horse for her.

She hadn't expected that he would ride with her. But again, she knew he valued his horses. He probably wanted to make sure she was right for Cinnamon instead of the other way around.

After a while, she laughed, and Mak glanced at her. "I just realized," she said. "I'm not quiet very often. But not talking makes me think the island is speaking to me. There seems to be a voice in the light wind and the sound of water gently caressing the sand. And it smells so good. What is that scent?"

"Jasmine," he said, and as they reached a rockier portion of the beach, he pointed out various foliage and called them by name. Some long stalks reminded her of the sugar cane fields they'd seen on Friday.

"Leia's grandparents are the Honeycutts who own the sugar plantation?" she asked.

"No. Her grandparents are Ari and Eeva Tane. They work at the plantation. My wife worked in the office primarily as book-keeper. Coming from a Hawaiian and Tahitian background, she knew the language as well as English. I saw her and thought her very beautiful." He paused. "Her parents warned her not to like me."

Mak glanced at her and apparently knew she was about to question that.

"The difference was class," he said. "They are workers. We are owners. They were afraid my friends would not accept Maylea."

"But they did, I'm sure," Jane said.

"If they had not, they would not be my friends."

She liked his adamant attitude. Of course, she knew about class distinction. No matter how much you valued another person, color or money stood in the way of relationships many times. Dread struck her. "Do you think the Honeycutts might not be so accepting of Pilar when they discover her mother has fallen from her social standing?"

He shook his head. "No. She is American. She will be highly favored by them. And she is a friend of Brother Russell's relatives. Here," he said and grinned, "that is high society."

That being settled, Jane stated the obvious. "But you married Maylea despite the objections."

She watched his face. It seemed to relax with a memory that did not seem so painful this time. "At a king's party, she and other young women performed the hula. Her brother is a well-known ukulele player. That was the night I knew I was in love with her. But at first she was very self-conscious, shy around me. You see, a lot of Hawaiians have been clothed with material and stripped of confidence in their culture and beliefs. The effects of that remains for generations. I wanted to know her beyond the shyness. I knew she was intelligent and educated. There's the class status, but that doesn't matter to me. An employer should be shown respect from their workers and vice versa. But one is not more worthy than another."

He looked over at her. "You apparently treat Pilar like family."

Jane still found that difficult to explain. "She and her mother worked for us, and there's a difference in roles. But here, we're responsible for her and certainly treat her as family. Oh, did you know that the school is talking about teaching the hula?"

He nodded. "It's language. The Hawaiians are starting to want some of their culture back, and the white man is starting to see it's not some forbidden, sensuous dance."

"But that's what attracted you to your wife."

"No," he said. "It wasn't just the hula. Other beautiful women were performing it, but I did not feel the same about them as I did about . . . Maylea." He paused. "I don't speak of her often. When I do, I usually refer to her as 'my wife.'"

"I can understand that a little," she said. "After Mama died, Dad didn't talk to me about her until Matilda noticed and made him do it. Matilda and I could talk about her and cry together." She shook her head. "But not Dad."

Mak nodded, and she thought that must be something men had in common.

"Something you said at the stable," he said, "remained in my mind. You said Panai might need a female friend. I took that rather personally."

"I didn't mean —"

"I hope you did." He paused as if uncertain about what to say. "I could use a woman friend. One I can talk to about . . . Maylea as I just did. I can't to Mother or Leia . . . to anyone. Everyone thinks I should be over it. But enough about me, Jane. Tell me about your fiancé. Quite rich,

I assume," he said with a smile, "being in oil."

CHAPTER 20

"Oh yes," Jane said truthfully. "The oil keeps gushing out like there's no end to it. It's exciting."

"Sounds as if you have a substantial future ahead," Mak said.

"Yes. I've been . . . very blessed." She gave him a quick look. That was nothing to be ashamed of. "My father has worked very hard to make the cattle ranch successful. His father started with almost nothing."

"What's your fiancé . . . what's his name?"

"Austin Price."

"What's he like?"

"Slippery when wet . . . with oil."

He laughed with her.

She looked out ahead, having a warm feeling talking about Austin. "He's very handsome. Has dark hair, warm gray eyes, tall, nice physique. About perfect in looks. And he's the nicest, kindest, finest man anywhere. We could talk about anything and everything. And most important, he's a committed Christian. Very generous with those less fortunate." She smiled over at Mak. "And a lot of fun."

"He sounds perfect," Mak said, and she noticed the lift of his eyebrows as if that were unbelievable. But he asked, "What does he do for fun?" He chuckled. "Other than debate with you."

She wasn't sure how to take that. "Oh, we have our card games and board games and charades. He's just good at conversation and making other people feel good. Never a negative word about anyone or anything. And the best thing, we would race each other on horseback."

"Who won?"

"Usually me."

"Did he let you win?"

She scoffed. "You are the most chauvinistic man. No, he didn't let me win." She leaned forward in a jockey stance. "I challenge you to a race."

"That horse doesn't stand a chance against Big Brown. She can hardly gallop."

"I thought as much," she said. "On foot, I could race this horse *on foot* and win."

She loved making him laugh. "Let me race you on Panai."

"Never."

The way he said that made her think she'd better change the subject, but he did first. "This thing bothers me," he said. "You were promised to Austin? I don't understand that."

"Oh, it was a pact between our parents. Or a hope, I guess would be more accurate. No one would hold us to that. I mean, neither of us ever found anyone who suited us better. Austin and I are different, but we complement each other."

"Is he your age?"

"Four years older. I'm twenty-three, twenty-four in March."

"Isn't that a long engagement?"

She looked out over the ocean, seeing surfers riding the waves far out. "Yes. I think it's about twenty-three-and-a-half years."

"Apparently you're in no hurry, if I'm not being too personal."

"Don't worry about being personal. I could lie at any time," she jested.

He punctuated his concurrence with a nod.

"But I did accept his ring on my eighteenth birthday. My friends were oohing and aahing. I became very excited about a big wedding. Then Aunt Matilda gave me a long talk. What I remember most was that she said it was fine to be excited about a big wedding. But just be sure I was planning a marriage, not simply a wedding." She glanced at Mak. "She wanted me to be sure I was in love with Austin and not just the idea of being in love and that I was ready to settle down."

"Sounds like a wise woman," he said.

"Very. I tried to visualize myself settled down." She shook her head. "I wasn't ready. I decided I wanted to be independent, travel like Matilda without asking my daddy or a husband for money and knowing he might refuse. So I began to teach horseback riding and equestrian classes. In case you haven't noticed, I'm a free spirit. I wasn't ready to be . . . tamed."

"Perhaps you shouldn't be. Like a racehorse. They need to be disciplined and trained, but not have their spirit broken."

"Oh," she said saucily, "and how do you train a girl like me?"

"That part is up to you, not someone else. One should not force another into some kind of mold but encourage them to recognize their strengths and weaknesses."

"That's how Austin feels. It's why he doesn't pressure me."

A hard look came over Mak's face. "That's something Maylea didn't understand. I wanted her to be herself. I loved who she was. But she wanted to be what she thought I would want, although I denied that. That's why she rode the spirited horse that day against my advice, trying to prove she was brave enough. I was always busy training my horses and taking care of the ranch, so she decided to teach Leia." He shook his head. "Of course the horse sensed her lack of confidence. Leia might have been fearful, too."

Jane realized she had said this before. "I'm so sorry."

He nodded. After a long silence, she asked, "What happened to the horse?"

She wondered if he'd ever reply. After a heavy sigh, he said, "The horse is Panai's mother. After the funeral and while Leia was still in the hospital, my foreman and paniolos had to hold me down to keep me from killing that animal. I threatened to fire them all, but they wouldn't let me go. Somebody took the horse away, and later, I found out the king bought her. He's raced her and won for the past three years. It's like having the horse laugh in my face."

Jane didn't know if she should say anything. They reached the end of the beach, and she turned Cinnamon back around when Mak turned Big Brown.

Bitterness was in his voice when he spoke

again. "The horse didn't care that my wife and unborn baby were killed. That Leia was hurt and lost her mother. That her parents are without their daughter. The world is without a beautiful, kind woman. The horse doesn't care. That's why Panai has to win that race. It's my revenge on the horse."

Jane asked tentatively, "You think the horse will know?"

He glanced at her. "I will know."

Jane wanted to reach over and touch his hand, make some physical gesture to show she cared. But he might resent that touch. He did not look receptive to any overture. What could she say, do? She uttered a silent prayer for guidance. But an answer did not form in her heart and mind.

"You've probably heard all kinds of explanations of why you shouldn't feel that way."

"Oh yes. Every possible reason — life, Satan, choices, one's time to go, accident, a better life in heaven." His voice was bitter. "You name it, I've heard it. But it doesn't make the pain go away. So you see, I have nothing of value to offer a woman. I only have . . . needs."

"Okay," she said. "Let's make a deal. I'll try and fulfill your need for a woman friend."

He sighed heavily. "I can't even be a friend

159

in return. I've turned into a grouch who I hardly recognize."

"Yes, you can be a friend. You have already, Mak. You've shared your home, your family, your *gentle* horse." She challenged him with a glance. "We could continue with you showing me the island."

Maybe he didn't want to show her the island. After a long moment, however, he said, "You've already made me realize I should talk to my daughter about her mother."

"Have you told her why she's afraid?"

"No, I wouldn't want Leia to blame her mother for putting her in danger."

"Mak, I heard that Maylea saved Leia's life."

It took a while before he acknowledged that with a nod. "Perhaps you could fill me in on how you would go about teaching Leia to ride. Was it your dad who taught you?"

"Oh yes. I was riding before I was walking, so I've been told. My mom tried to teach me to be a lady." She wrinkled her nose, and Mak grinned. "My dad wanted a boy, so that may be why he taught me to care for animals and ride like a man. I needed those equestrian lessons to teach me how to ride like a lady."

He laughed when she said *lady* as if it were

unsavory.

Then he surprised her by saying, "How do you go about teaching that to a child?"

"Easy," she said. "Sit erect and wear a stylish riding habit."

At the skeptical look he gave her, she laughed. "That's the lady part. The first thing I do is lead the children to the stall, have them take a rake, and go apple-picking in the straw."

"Apple-picking? Why would apples be in the stall? The horses would eat them."

"That's the word my daddy used for cleaning out the stall. The horse's apples would be chucked into a pail."

He grimaced. "You'd have a child do that?"

She looked him in the face. "Of course. A rider needs to know how to keep his horse's stall clean, even if they have their own stable boys. That's the first lesson. If parents aren't willing to have the child learn complete care of a horse, then I won't take the child on as a student."

He looked away, and she figured that was the end of that. "You see, after a child does the dirtiest, smelliest job, then keeping the animal clean is not at all a dirty job, but a pleasure."

The lift of his eyebrows and a brief nod

indicated he agreed.

"Next," she said, "I have the child learn to feel the horse, get used to him, and allow the horse to get used to the child's touch and voice." Remembering that his wife was thrown, she said, "I also teach a child how to fall, to be prepared to hold onto the reins or grab the saddle horn, anticipate that even the most gentle horse can be frightened, perhaps by a snake in the road."

His quick laugh made her think he didn't care for her methods. The grin stayed on his face when he said, "There are no snakes in Hawaii."

Shocked, her jaw dropped. "No snakes? Not one?"

"Nope. The only things here are what people from other countries have brought in. None have brought any snakes."

While she was trying to recover from that disclosure, he said, "If you could get my little lady to . . . pick apples, you could get her to do anything."

CHAPTER 21

Pilar squealed, "No!"

Uncle Russell said, "Well, well."

Matilda nodded while she stared at Jane.

They'd each gotten mail. Jane hadn't read her second letter yet.

"Bet I know what this is about," Matilda had said when Uncle Russell brought the letters home. Letters didn't usually come for all of them at the same time. They'd settled at the kitchen table, each looking at the envelopes until Matilda had said, "We have to open them sometime."

"They're coming?" Pilar said. "Is that what your letters say?"

"They're already on their way. They should be here in February."

Pilar began to wail. "I don't want to go back. I don't ever want to leave here. I mean . . ." She stood and held onto the edge of the table while they all stared at her. "I can't go back to being my mother's helper, anymore. Jane, you'll be married. Matilda won't be there. I have plans. I have friends here. It's not like in Texas."

She threw her letter on the table and ran from the room.

"I'll talk to her later," Matilda said.

"I understand her wanting to stay here," Jane said. "But I can't see Inez allowing it. Where would she stay, anyway?"

"She's welcome here," Uncle Russell said. "But although I'm a preacher, her mother doesn't know me and might not agree."

At suppertime, Pilar brought the subject up again. "I'll have to do what my mother says, won't I? After I graduate from school, I could get a job. Maybe in the sugar fields." She shook her head. "That wouldn't work. Susanne wouldn't be my friend if I worked for her parents." She looked quickly at Jane. "I don't mean that you're not because I worked for your dad."

"I know that, Pilar. There's six years difference in your age and mine, so the situation isn't the same. Maybe your mother will fall in love with Hawaii, too, and want to stay."

Pilar exhaled heavily. "My mother doesn't fall in love with anything. She just wants to stay a cook and a housekeeper."

Matilda reached over and laid her hand

on Pilar's. "Your mother takes pride in her work, Pilar. That's about all she has." She patted the girl's hand. "I'll reason with her."

"But she doesn't . . . I mean . . ."

"I know what you mean," Matilda said. "Your mother feels stuck in a kitchen while I gallivant all over the world. It's not really me she dislikes. I mean, if my husband hadn't left me a pile of money, I'd be spitting on his grave twenty-five times a day."

A hopeful look came into Pilar's eyes. "You can make her understand about me. You can do anything."

"Pretty much," Matilda agreed. "Now stop your worrying."

After supper, as Jane and Matilda walked toward the church, Jane remembered what Matilda had implied before they left Texas. "You don't think Inez . . . and my dad . . . ?"

"Oh yes, I do. I have a feeling they're going to make an announcement, and Pilar's plight will be secondary. Oh, I don't mean they won't care, but if there's some reasonable way they feel Pilar has a better future in Hawaii than in Texas, they'll likely consent. I'm sure I can help in some way. There's no place I have to be in a hurry."

Jane threw her arms around Matilda. "I love you, Matilda. It's amazing how you can be so independent and yet care enough to be right there to help when someone needs it."

Matilda smiled. "Did you ever stop to think, Jane dear, I need it, too? I need your love. I need the feeling of being wanted and needed. I think that's why the good Lord admonished us to help each other."

"I've always known that," Jane said. "But I've mostly been on the receiving end. I don't want to be selfish, and I like the feeling of having been some help to Pansy and to Uncle Russell."

"You were always just fine, Jane. But you have matured in many ways since we've been here. We aren't born wise; we grow into it."

"I hope so. And you know, I think I can be a real help to Mak. He's opened up to me a little. And after things I've heard from you and Rose and Uncle Russell, he hasn't done that since his wife died." She stopped and caught hold of Matilda's hands. "I'm going Saturday morning to talk to him about how I would teach Leia. I know he'll be testing me, but I think this is a big hurdle for him to overcome. I so want to be helpful."

"That's good, Jane," she said, giving her hands a squeeze, then letting go. "But in the meantime, don't you think you need to give your dad and Austin some thought? In about three months they'll be here."

"Three months," Jane mused. "That's enough time to get Leia riding like a girl her age should. Time to get Mak to realize he needs to accept his wife's death and move on with his life. You know, he's stuck in the day she died. He just can't let it go. Maybe we can even get him back in church."

"Jane."

Jane turned her head to stare at Matilda.

"In three months, your dad and Austin will be here."

"Oh my," Jane said. "I feel like I'm just getting a good grasp of my land legs. Now I have to start thinking about my sea legs?" Of course, her attention would need to revert from Mak's needs to Austin.

As if reading her mind, Matilda said, "Now dear. Do we plan a Hawaiian wedding . . . or what?"

CHAPTER 22

Dressed in her least stylish riding pants, Jane eagerly awaited Friday when Mak would finish his classes and they'd ride together to his ranch.

"Let's stop in town and pick up something to eat," he said after the school let out for lunch. At the colorful farmer's market, Jane again felt much like a minority, seeing the food and wares of Japanese, Portuguese, Polynesian, Korean, and Chinese people. She and Mak each settled for a cinnamon-raisin-macadamia-nut shortbread cookie, and divided one for each horse. She learned of fruits that were foreign to her — lychee, lilikoi, star fruit, guava.

"I know banana," she teased.

"Probably not this kind," he said. "There are about fourteen varieties in Hawaii."

After munching on the delicious cookies, they mounted the horses and headed for a trot-walk to the ranch. Mak confided, "I did tell Leia that her fear stems from her knowing her mother was thrown from a horse. But I didn't feel the time was right for going into further detail."

Jane felt that was progress. When she and Mak rode up, she wasn't surprised to see Rose and Leia waiting outside the carriage house. As she followed Mak into the corral where they left Big Brown and Cinnamon, he murmured, "I've never before seen my daughter in pants." He took a deep breath. "Nor my mother looking quite so triumphant."

"Where did you get that outfit?" Mak said, walking up to them.

"Aloha, Jane," Rose said with a big smile before answering Mak, while Leia pulled the sides of her pants like a girl curtsying in a skirt. "Chico borrowed the pants from one of the paniolos' sons who's about Leia's size."

Mak was seeing his little lady in old-looking shoes and the clothes of the son of a cowboy who worked for him. Jane however, could visualize Leia in a real riding outfit and boots.

Rose leaned toward Jane and spoke softly. "The boy has worn these pants many times for the same purpose." Then she addressed them all. "I'll leave this to you. Later, I'll serve some refreshments."

Jane looked at her and mumbled, "No apples," and they both laughed.

Rose walked toward the house, still chuckling.

Jane knew the next few minutes were critical. With one knee bent and a booted foot braced against the wall, Mak leaned back with his arms folded while Jane explained the process to Leia.

Leia crinkled her nose. "But Daddy, you don't like for me to get dirty."

He scoffed. "Has that ever stopped you?"

Jane knew this could end the session before it even started. But she couldn't, wouldn't back down on that point. Of course, stable boys could clean the stalls. But this was an important part of discipline and the care of an animal. Long before now, Leia should have been accustomed to all parts of animal behavior. Jane had certainly learned the hard way about cow patties. She continued holding onto the rake.

Mak could change his mind in a moment, too. His next words indicated that. "No, you don't have to, Leia. Miss Jane said that many young girls in Texas have drivers who take them where they need to go. Or they can wait until their dad or family member feels like taking them into town or on excursions."

Her lip poked out. "I want to do it myself."

He said, "There's only one way."

Her eyes challenged her dad and Jane, but neither spoke. Her lips tightened, but she came over to Jane and took the pitchfork. Jane reached for another one.

Leia gasped. "You're going to do it, too?"

"Certainly. It's just part of being in your horse's life."

"Okay," she said, as if beginning to play a game. "Let's see who picks the most apples."

"Okay," Jane said back. "Just don't toss any the wrong way."

Mak watched, astounded. His little girl was helping clean out Big Brown's stall. Early that morning, he had told the bewildered stable boy to leave some of the apples in the stall.

Even so, he never would have thought such a thing could happen, or that it should. But Leia, to his surprise, stuck with the job. She and Jane would make sounds like "P-uewee" and turn their heads, then laugh.

How good to hear a woman laugh with his child. Of course, his mother often did, but he was used to that. This was different. Reminded him again of Maylea and what he and Leia both missed.

Strange, he thought more highly of Jane picking apples than when she stood around looking like a beautiful lady. She wasn't above getting downright smelly and messy. She was teaching his daughter, a young girl of privilege, what it meant to work. And his daughter seemed happier with that than when his mother was teaching her to crochet.

Well, Miss Jane could often look like a dainty, well-bred creature, but she sure knew how to clean out a stall, like a man . . . or rather, like a stable boy.

When they finished, Jane walked over to him. "You don't have any airs about you, Miss Jane," he said and watched her smile disappear and a warning look come into her eyes when he added, "except what might linger after a stall cleaning."

"Well, for your information, I love the smell of horses and stables."

Leia's smile looked more like a grimace, but she didn't dispute that.

"Now," Jane said. "For the next step."

He planted both feet on the floor. "A horse?"

"Exactly."

His little girl, or rather *stable girl,* put her hands together like she might applaud.

172

"Miss Jane," he said, "Do you think Cinnamon would do?"

"You mean that nice, sweet, gentle, trot-walking horse?"

"Exactly."

Jane nodded. "Bring her in."

Mak listened to what Jane was saying to Leia, who had wanted to ride for a long time. Now in the presence of such a big horse, she seemed shy, and he knew that moment of imbedded fear would surface.

"He's your pet, Leia," Jane said, "but not just a pet. He's also your transportation, and you must always be in control of him. You must learn to train him to do what you want. Don't let him do whatever he wants."

Leia was nodding. "That sounds like what Daddy and Grandmother tell me. They make me do what they want. Dry the dishes. Clean my room. Wash my hands." She lifted her hands. "On and on."

"That's so you will grow up to be a properly trained, obedient, fine young lady."

Leia looked at the apple pail in the corner. "Ladies pick that kind of apples?"

"Oh yes. I'm a lady, and I just did it."

"Does Miss Tilda?"

"She has when she took care of her own horses. She would again if she needed to. Young ladies do many things. Some sit in drawing rooms and knit or crochet."

Seeing Leia's nose begin to crinkle, Mak thought she wasn't too fond of that.

"Others enjoy outdoor activities," Jane was saying. "But you need to know how to do all things."

"I want to be a lady." His daughter looked very serious. "Like you."

"Okay," Jane said. "Now introduce yourself to Cinnamon. After that, I'll show you how to touch her. It's fine to touch her gently, but at other times you should touch her firmly. Like your daddy would hold your hand firmly to cross a street if a horse and carriage was coming toward you real fast."

Her eyebrows lifted. "He would pick me up and run."

"Okay, let's see you try to pick up Cinnamon."

Even Mak laughed at that.

He was seeing how excited Leia was about all this. Even at her young age, Leia was not content staying indoors, doing what he considered *safe* things. But how could she be? Her mother came from hardworking laborers on a sugar plantation whose ancestors had taken an uncertain ocean voyage. His parents were adventurers who had left their country to make Hawaii their home.

He was beginning to see some of the

things his mother had tried to tell him about his own daughter. But he'd been helpless about what to do. Soon she came to say refreshments were ready any time they were.

"I think you need to get cleaned up first," his mother said to Leia. They walked ahead, with Leia telling his mother what she did and what she learned.

Jane looked up at Mak. "I would never have thought a horse like Big Brown could leave a stall so clean overnight."

She had a way of observing the minutest of things. "And I would never have thought a child could win an apple-picking game over an accomplished horsewoman."

"Okay," she said, "I guess that means we're both devious."

"Or," he said, "both trying to do what's best for a child."

"So the lesson went well?"

He nodded. "Better than I expected."

"You mean you didn't expect much from me?" She placed her hands on her hips.

He stopped in front of her, looking at his mother and daughter to see if they were out of hearing range. "I didn't expect my daughter to clean out a stall. I admit I don't know her as well as I thought I did." He inhaled and looked over her head for a moment.

"Leia is a strong-willed, adventurous little girl."

"That isn't bad, Mak."

He'd heard Jane describe herself that way. He reached up and brushed aside a stray lock of hair the wind blew against her cheek. "No. Not bad at all."

Her expression showed surprise. Was that because he'd touched her or was it his admitting that adventurous wasn't bad? She slapped the leg of her pants. "I just realized something," she said. "I don't have a horse. Cinnamon needs to be here for Leia to talk to and feed oats and apples."

"She learned a lot today. Thank you."

"You're welcome. But I learned something, too. Your bringing Cinnamon to me had nothing whatsoever do with the color of my eyes or my hair. You wanted to find out if I thought the horse would be right for Leia."

He shrugged. What could he say?

"Mak, you could have told me that."

They'd neared the house, so he stopped again and stood in front of her. "I wasn't trying to be deceptive. I wasn't sure about allowing Leia to learn. It's like this is all happening, unfolding, when I didn't really plan it."

Would she understand that? After a moment she said, "Could this be one of those times Uncle Russell talked about when he said the Lord works in mysterious ways?"

She stared into his eyes. After a long moment, he turned and walked on. "I don't know," he said seriously. "Most of God's ways are a mystery to me." He opened the screen door. "But I'll get you another horse."

Her eyes widened, and her voice sounded incredulous. "One that can really gallop?"

She could make him laugh more in a few minutes than anyone else had done . . . in a long time.

CHAPTER 23

Jane thought he might choose the white horse for her, but when he didn't, she figured he thought it might be a mite too frisky. After they returned to the stables he asked a stable boy to bring Anise to the corral.

She loved the horse the moment she saw her. Mak had chosen a beautiful brown mare with a black mane and tail, not as large as Big Brown or as old, but a fine, strong animal. Maybe he did respect her ability as a horsewoman.

"Shall we gallop out and see how Panai is doing with his workout?" he asked.

"I'd love that."

"Just remember," he said as they mounted the horses. "Don't try to ride like the wind before you and the horse relate well. Like you told Leia, you need to know each other first."

Jane felt so good in the saddle, like the

two of them were made for each other. "I promise," she said. "I will not ride like the wind." She gave him a sly look. "Like a Texas tornado wind, that is."

He gave her a warning look. "Just try to hold it down to a gentle Hawaiian breeze for now."

As they cantered across the velvety green range, Jane mentioned that her dad, Austin, and Inez were coming to the island. "They will probably arrive in February."

After a moment, he said, "Oh, in wintertime."

"What's winter like here?"

He sighed as if that were a problem. "About two degrees cooler and a few more inches of rain."

She laughed as he smiled at her.

"I'm sure that seems like a long way off for you."

"Long enough for me to help Leia get over her fear and learn how to properly care for horses, get them to trust and obey."

He scoffed. "That sounds rather religious."

Jane smiled. "Well, aren't we humans sometimes rather like wild horses? The Lord has to rein us in."

His head turned toward her, and his eyes held a curious look. "You don't strike me as a wild horse."

"Well I shouldn't tell you this, but Billy and I went out behind the barn to smoke one of my daddy's cigars. But first, I grabbed Billy and I kissed him right on the lips."

"No," Mak said, feigning shock. "How old were you?"

"Fourteen."

He laughed heartily.

"That's funny?"

"I was remembering the description Reverend gave me of you at fourteen."

"And that's funny?"

"He did describe you as . . . a child. I can't imagine that kiss being anything like a wild horse."

"Well, we experimented with a few more kisses. That's before we sat with our backs against the barn and began taking turns with the cigar."

"Ahhh." His eyebrows lifted. "Now you're beginning to get sinful."

She laughed at the teasing. "Oh, we paid the consequences for that. You see, that's when I learned the meaning of a sick stomach."

She liked his laugh. "And when I got off that ship here in Hawaii, the reminder returned. I so wanted to make a good impression."

"You did make an indelible one," he said. "Unforgettable." He chuckled. "Now I know how sinful you are."

"Oh," she boasted. "That was only the beginning. I determined to kiss at least two boys at every church social, every party, or whenever I got the chance." She lowered her head. "But of course, I had to pretend it was their idea so I wouldn't get a bad reputation."

"Why two?" he asked.

"I have always been promised to Austin. Aunt Matilda taught me that I had to consider other possibilities, and I thought a kiss would be the best way."

"And Austin always won?"

"He wasn't always the best kisser, but he was always the best man."

She figured turnabout was fair play, so she asked, "How old were you when you had your first kiss?"

He gazed out across the land. "Twelve? No, eleven. Yes. Eleven."

"Eleven kisses, or eleven years old?"

He shrugged and glanced at her. "Both. She was a cutie. Brown as a Kona coffee bean. Big brown eyes. Almost all eyes and lips. You know?" He made finger motions at his own lips as if trying to draw heart-shaped ones.

Jane nodded.

"But she wouldn't let me kiss her lips. Only her cheeks. She said her mother told her not to let a boy kiss her lips." He sighed. "Just being near them was heaven. On about the twelfth kiss, I made a mistake and kissed her lips. I think I was twelve by then."

"Mistake?"

He nodded. "She ran away. Never let me kiss her again."

Jane moaned, and when he glanced at her she frowned, trying to appear sad. "Oh, the consequences of being wild horses."

"Maybe we weren't so bad. Just children."

Jane realized his mood had gone from playfulness to serious. What had he been thinking? Three years without a kiss from his wife? Of course he missed that. Her closeness, her love.

"You were just a child when you lost your mother, weren't you?" he asked.

"My mother was killed in a tornado. She was a schoolteacher. The school collapsed. She had herded the children into the storm cellar beneath the school. I was one of those children. But she didn't make it."

"You know loss. Yet you seem so happy. Is it time that does it?"

"Matilda made me cry and grieve. She's

known many losses. But through the years, she has taught me that people are different. Some are uptight, and some are . . ." She turned her face toward him until he looked. "Some are free spirits."

He smiled. "I think there's more to it."

"Sure there is. But I can't teach you everything about life in only one day."

He laughed. "We'll just have to have classes together, teacher." He paused. "Speaking of teaching, my mother thinks I should have Leia in the mission school. I've thought she was better off being tutored by my mother. But I'm beginning to think she may be right. Leia begs me to let her go there. You've been a girl and without a mother. What do you think?"

"I think, Mak, that you're having as much trouble letting go of Leia as you are with letting go of . . . your wife."

At his surprised expression, Jane apologized. "I'm sorry. I shouldn't have said that."

He gave her a long look. "Why did you?"

"Because," she said, afraid she had just alienated him. "Sometimes my tongue is as uncontrollable as tumbleweed in a windstorm."

He looked at her quickly. "I have no idea what you're saying. Tumbleweed?"

"Tumbleweed is a plant. The wind breaks

it off from the roots and rolls it along wherever it will. So what I mean is I talk a lot and sometimes say the wrong thing."

They trotted along for quite a while. She feared he'd tell her to turn around and go back to town. He finally said, "Jane, I've said we could be friends and that we can talk about what's important to us. I've had so many people tell me how I should feel and not feel, that I'm afraid I have a short temper where that's concerned. I'm sorry."

"Okay. Do you still want my opinion?"

He grinned. "Go ahead. I'll hang on tight in case a tumbleweed heads my way."

She began. "We both know I can't tell you what to do. But it would be nice, I think, if Rose could be more like a grandmother. She can fill a mother's role but can never replace her. Matilda was my wonderful, wonderful aunt, and we both have benefited from that. And the school seems to be a really fine school. The children are happy, the teachers are caring . . . ahem."

His puzzled look changed to understanding. "Thank you, Miss Buckley," he said with mock formality. "But this teacher is temporary. I don't intend to return after Christmas holidays and may leave sooner if Russell gets a replacement. Besides, it's a long way for Leia to go to school."

"She could stay home and be taught by you or your mother in bad weather."

His expression was amused. "We don't have bad weather."

"Oh yes. I forgot. This is paradise."

"Right," he said. "We only have tidal waves, earthquakes, and volcanic eruptions."

CHAPTER 24

"By the way," Jane said, realizing they were headed in a different direction than town. "Where are we going?"

Mak brought Big Brown to a halt. "Sorry. I'm assuming instead of asking. Would you like to see more of the ranch?"

She gave him a big smile. "I was afraid you were escorting me home. Tell you what. Let's just be really honest, and if one of us starts to take advantage of the other's time or anything, just say so. How's that?"

He took off his hat and held it against his heart, causing the breeze to stir the waves of his hair. "It's a deal. Would you like to see Panai's workout?"

"Look at it this way, Mak MacCauley. If you came to Texas and knew my daddy had a ranch, would you want to go see an oil well?"

With a grin, he returned the hat to his head. The next thing she knew, Big Brown had responded to his leg and hand motion and they were galloping across the green grass.

"One of these days," he said, "we might stroll through a field of lava and walk along the black sand beaches."

"Ach." She pulled the horse to a halt.

Mak stopped. "What's wrong?"

"You just said the strangest thing I ever heard in my life."

"What? What did I say?"

"You said we'd walk through lava."

He shrugged. "So?"

"That's worse than if I would say, 'Let's stroll along the lawn, amidst the cow patties, and listen to the mooing.' "

When he could stop laughing, he said with irony, "Ah, our different worlds. Yes, I suppose you're right. But I bet you my lava setting is more appealing than your cow-patty one."

"Prove it," she teased.

"I can." Then he surprised her by taking Big Brown into a fast gallop.

"I'll catch up," she called, bringing Anise to a trot while she took the pins from her hair and loosened it with her fingers.

Mak slowed and looked over his shoulder. She fast-galloped up to him, and they rode side by side. He kept looking over, and his eyes seemed to linger on her long hair blowing out from her head like the tail of a horse.

"Ahhh," she said.

He pushed his hat back so it lay between his shoulders, ran the fingers of one hand through his dark hair, then grimaced. "Not the same," he said.

She laughed. Was that some kind of off-hand compliment?

The stables, corral, and bunkhouse came into view first. Several men were tending the horses. Cattle and horses grazed in the open fields beyond, but with a wave of their hands, she and Mak kept riding.

Jane was speechless. Lying ahead was a fenced racetrack so huge she couldn't see the end of it. Chico was leading Panai in a slow trot over to the fence. Jane was off Anise before Mak could dismount.

"Careful," Mak warned as Panai stuck his head over the top of the white wooden fence.

"He's inviting me to come over," she said as Chico dismounted.

"You're right," Chico said, climbing over the fence with a broad smile that creased his browned face.

Two other men walked up, and Mak introduced them. She learned that Tomas was one of Mak's trainers and Clint was the ranch's foreman. The men seemed to already have heard about her, mentioned her uncle Russell, took off their hats at the mention of Pansy, and asked a couple questions about her daddy's Texas ranch.

After a moment, Clint said he needed to get back to work. "The boss might catch me loafing." The next moment, he was galloping off on his horse.

Chico made a strange sound like a grunt, and his hand moved to his stomach as he bent over a few inches.

"Chico?" Mak said. "Something wrong?"

Chico's hand dropped to his side, and he straightened. His face took on an innocent look, but it seemed to have lost its healthy glow. "No. Why?"

Jane saw Mak look at Tomas, who gazed off across the racetrack like he wasn't even listening.

"Don't lie to me," Mak said, giving Chico a hard look.

Chico shrugged. "It's only an upset stomach. The cook made pancakes this morning, and it's just too heavy in my stomach to eat that and come ride. I'll change my way of living."

Chico laughed as if it were nothing.

Mak didn't. "I've never known you to have a sick day in your life, Chico. But I don't want you on Panai if you're ill. Tomas here can ride Panai and get somebody to keep the time. If you need to see a doctor, see a doctor."

"I will, Mr. Mak. Now, I need to take Panai around one more time."

When Mak looked at him skeptically, Jane stuck her arm over the fence rails and rubbed the horse's neck. "Let me ride him."

Mak didn't bother to laugh. "No woman has ever been on that horse."

She was looking in Panai's eyes. "He would let me ride him."

"He's not just a horse. He's a trained racer."

Drawing in a deep breath she lifted her chin. "So am I."

At his withering stare, she corrected that. "Well, not the kind you and Chico are. But I've raced my dad. And as an equestrienne, I've not only ridden with speed but had the horse jump" — she measured with her hand — "This high." She added, "I've even won awards."

There it was again. That sinking feeling that she'd never come in first.

He stuck one booted foot on a rail, swung the other up, and over the fence he went. She did the same. "Let me ride with you."

He mounted the horse, and by that time,

Tomas had climbed over and helped Mak lift her onto the horse.

"I don't believe this," Mak murmured.

Jane looked at the two silent men, both bug-eyed like they didn't believe it, either.

"No timing," Mak said to Tomas. "Just call it a . . . workout."

"Oh you beautiful, beautiful, wonderful horse," Jane told Panai, leaning over his magnificent mane. "You like me here, don't you?"

Mak started him off slowly, knowing it was a test for them all. Jane wasn't concerned about herself or Panai but wondered what emotion the horse might sense from Mak. But he knew Mak as his master. She knew Panai didn't want to trot, then canter, then gallop. He wanted to fly.

As Mak allowed the horse more free rein, she felt the power, the warmth, the strength, the determination. And that's what she felt sitting in front of Mak with his arms around her. She knew his total focus was on the horse.

She tried to make it hers, but her silly brain kept feeling the warmth of his body leaning against hers, the strength of his arms around her, the sound of his voice touching the top of her head as if it were entering through her hair, and it affected her mind as he talked to Panai, saying, "Let's hold back. Save the best for the race, Panai. Good boy."

She was flying. Faster than she'd ever flown in her life. Lifted higher than she'd ever been. The wind was in her face. The scenery sped by like a green ribbon. Nothing existed but the wish that this feeling of being completely unfettered might last forever.

It ended too soon.

"How was it?" Mak said, dismounting and lifting his arms to her.

Her chest heaved with excitement. "Exhilarating." As her feet touched the ground with his hands at her waist, she instinctively wrapped her arms around him, her head against his chest. His heart was thundering, too. "Thank you. Thank you."

"Do you have your land legs?" he said, taking hold of her arms.

She shouldn't have done that. But so much was going through her mind. She'd just had the ride of her life. She felt tears of joy smart her eyes, and she climbed over the fence to reality.

Later, after riding back to town — without Mak feeling he had to escort her — she could hardly wait to tell Matilda all about it. After gushing like an oil well about the ride, she said, "I felt so free, Matilda. Sometimes, looking at this ring and thinking about marriage, I think I may not be ready. And this is such a breakthrough that Mak allows a woman — a single woman — to be near him."

Matilda shook her head. "Don't forget, dear. The reason you're allowed to ride that horse, to be near Mak, is because you're wearing that ring."

CHAPTER 25

"Oh, I'll never get the syllables right," Jane wailed. "I keep saying *Kalimikika* or *Keli ki ka ma* instead of *Kali . . . Kali . . .*" She threw up her hands. "What's the use?"

"What's the use?" Matilda gave her a studied look. "We may need to say it to the queen. Or more important, to children. Now, Rose taught me how to say it, and you girls can learn, too. Let's try word association." She took a deep breath. "Think of this sentence: My cart is leaky from spilled milk while I'm riding in my cart."

Jane's eyes swung to Pilar, who was shaking her head and covering her mouth to hold back the laughter. Matilda ignored it. "Now think 'cart leaky, my cart,' but instead of 'my' say 'ma' and instead of cart say 'ca.' "

"Okay." Jane could hardly get the words out while holding her stomach from the laughter that filled her body. "My horse is leaking while pulling Ma's cart."

Pilar cleared her throat. "My ma doesn't have a cart, and I don't think she leaks."

Matilda slapped her hands down on the kitchen table. "Oh, you girls are impossible. Now try this. *Kart-liki ma-cart.*"

Jane and Pilar spoke in unison. *"Cart-leaky, ma-cart. Cart-leaky ma-cart."*

Matilda moved her hand like waving a baton. "Not bad. Leave out the *r* and *t. Ka-likimaka.*"

"Ca-leaky ma-ca."

"Perfect. Now add the *Mele* in front of it and you have *Merry Christmas.*"

Uncle Russell walked into the kitchen, laughing. "You could just say *Merry Christmas.* Everybody understands that."

"Oh Russ," Matilda chided. "We're in Hawaii. The Bible says when in Rome do as the Romans do."

"It does?" He pulled out a chair. "This isn't an exact translation," he said, sitting. "But a phonetic translation. When Christmas first came to the islands, the Hawaiians had difficulty pronouncing *Merry Christmas.* Think about the pronunciation here. It sounds a lot like *Merry Christmas.*"

"Now why didn't you say that, Matilda?" Jane jested. "That makes it so much easier. She jumped up and hurried to the door. "I think I hear their wagon."

The rest of them followed. Mak had some of his men take the farm wagon up in the mountains and bring down Christmas trees and cypress boughs to decorate the school and church. Sure enough, there was Mak driving the farm wagon.

Before they got Uncle Russell's tree unloaded and the boards nailed onto the trunk, Rose and Leia drove up in a horse-drawn cart loaded with greenery and boxes.

A couple other wagons pulled up. This was the day to decorate Uncle Russell's house, the church, and the school.

When Rose and Mak came in with cardboard boxes, Jane tried out her new words. "Mele . . ." She thought, *My cart is leaking.* "Maca leaky."

Mak smiled broadly. "Merry Mas-Christ to you, too. And a *Hau'oli Makahiki Hou.*"

She stomped her foot. "I'm going to forget Christmas altogether." Then she gasped with pleasure as Leia opened a box lid and exposed bright red, silk flowers they would use to make leis. "Oh, I just got an extra dose of Christmas spirit."

They left some of the greenery at the house, went to the church, and unloaded more. Uncle Russell directed them to a closet where last year's decorations had been stored.

"Pansy packed them away," he said. "She labeled all the boxes."

Leia piped up. "She will have Christmas with the baby Jesus." She looked at Jane. "Is that right?"

Jane had begun going to the ranch three mornings a week for Leia's lessons. She was also telling her about the difference between the myths about Little People and the truth about Jesus.

"Yes, she will celebrate Jesus' birthday in heaven, and we will celebrate it here. By the way, do you know about . . ." She was reluctant to say it. "Santa?"

"Oooh." Leia clapped her hands. "Yes, I saw Santa another Christmas. He brings presents." Her eyes grew big and excited. Then a worry line formed above her nose. "Is he a Jesus story or a Little People story?"

Jane looked to the men who had nailed the wooden pieces to the bottom of the tree trunk and set it on the stage. Mak glanced over his shoulder at her, as if wondering what she'd say. Rose and Matilda were hanging garland. They didn't offer to answer. Okay, she'd try.

"It's a story, like the stories of the Little People." She looked around, hoping to signal the others to step in at any moment because she wasn't even sure what she would say. "Santa is a symbol, like Little People are a symbol. Do you know what a symbol is?"

Leia shook her head.

"It's like the lei is a symbol of Hawaii. You greeted me with one. It's welcoming me to Hawaii. Santa is a symbol of someone giving gifts because God gave us the gift of His Son, Jesus, to the world."

Leia smiled. "Okay."

That seemed a little too easy. Looking around, Jane saw that others smiled. They seemed to think it was okay.

Good. She'd take it further. "In America, Santa comes down the chimney."

"The chimney?"

Mak tossed out, "We don't have chimneys here."

"What's a chimney?" Leia wanted to know.

"Well," she said to the eager little girl. "There's a fireplace where we burn logs and the smoke goes up the chimney."

"Won't he get burned up?"

"He doesn't really do that. It's just part of the story."

"Oh," Leia said. "Santa could come down our stovepipe. If he was" — she brought her hands close together — "about this big, like the Little People."

When nobody disagreed, Leia added, "He would be a little symbol."

"Okay," Jane said. Maybe Leia wasn't ready for theology.

When Leia delivered an ornament to Rose, Mak stepped up to Jane. "Not bad," he said, "for a woman."

She jested, "Maybe you should dress up like Santa and make the message clearer."

"Not a bad idea. Maybe next year."

Jane felt good about him. He was making an effort to become more involved with people and his own family. Yes, maybe next year . . . a lot of changes would have taken place.

The thought hit her like a thunderbolt.

Next year.

What would she be doing next year?

Jane looked down, and her gaze landed on her ring. Next year, would she be in the U.S.A., celebrating Christmas as Mrs. Austin Price?

CHAPTER 26

Although Hawaii had its mountain topped with snow and a volcano spewing fire, the town and Mak's ranch were situated in the green valley where temperatures remained pleasant. The sun kept shining even when a light misty rain fell.

"It's not going to be a cold Christmas," Jane said somewhat wistfully as she sat around Uncle Russell's kitchen table with Matilda, Pilar, Rose, and Leia making silk leis.

"That doesn't slow down the celebration," Rose assured her. "Everybody comes out to celebrate on Christmas Eve."

"It wasn't always that way," Uncle Russell said, pouring himself a cup of coffee. "The Hawaiians worshiped false gods."

"I guess the early missionaries brought Christmas to the islands," Matilda said. "Come sit down." She gestured to the chair near the table. "We can scoot."

"Wouldn't want to chance spilling this coffee on those leis," he said. "I'm fine." He moved the chair back farther and sat in it. "The early missionaries brought the message of Jesus and salvation. But the Puritans had left England for religious purposes. They were against some of the customs and revelry that flourished in Europe. Since the Bible didn't teach anything about Christmas, they didn't even talk or preach about it. They brought Christianity to the islands, but not Christmas."

"So how did it come about?" Jane asked.

"Inevitably some whalers, business people, and travelers from other countries would be here at Christmastime. They would celebrate and give gifts, and the word got around that was another way the white man worshiped his God."

"But you say it's a big thing now?" Matilda said.

"Yes, the king can be credited with that. About thirty-five years ago, long before Pansy and I came here, the king had spent Christmas in Europe. When he came back, he declared Thanksgiving as a national day to be celebrated on December 25. But since most people on the island are now Christians, they consider December 25 as a celebration of the birth of Jesus Christ."

Rose commented, "And it's grown bigger every year. It's really spectacular."

"Yes," Leia said. "I'm bigger, and I'm going to sing in the choir."

"So are we all," Matilda said. "Not in the children's choir."

"So am I," said Pilar with a big smile. "And Susanne."

Despite the beautiful weather and the mist that the others called rain, Jane got caught up in the spirit of Christmas. The house looked festive, and they made plans for food and parties, including one for Leia on Christmas Day.

"What we ladies need to do," Matilda said, "is go downtown for lunch and go shopping. I'll treat."

"Yes, yes!" Leia was about to come off her seat.

"Sounds like a great idea," Uncle Russell said. "I'll just take myself a nap and later on get to work on my Christmas Eve sermon."

Unable to decide where to have lunch, Rose made a suggestion. "Why don't we order a couple of plates and sample various foods?"

They entered the first in a line of Hilo restaurants and soon dipped into a bowl of Hawaiian Portuguese bean soup and fresh fish caught right at the shore and flavored with ginger, soy, and garlic. "I must try breadfruit," Jane said. "Are people looking at us funny?"

"No, no," Rose assured them. "This is what all visitors or newcomers to Hawaii do. They just think you're Americans or Europeans."

"Oh," Matilda scoffed. "I thought I would be inconspicuous in this *muumuu.*"

They all laughed. Matilda stood out in any crowd. They had all decided to wear muumuus, a casual style of island dress that was lighter and looser than western dress. Rose lent Matilda one. Jane purchased one from a store. Her preference however was pants, since she was riding not only to the ranch several times a week but also along the beach and along trails bordered by lush foliage.

After lunch, they walked down the street and saw a couple of boys staring in the candy store window and singing. "Oh, they're singing a song we made up at school," Pilar said. "Do you know it, Leia?"

"Some of it," she said.

The two girls walked up to the boys, and with all four putting forth their best efforts, they were finally satisfied with their chant:

Candies red as a sunset sky
Cakes that please the tongue and eye
Sugared flowers not for a lei
But for children on Christmas Day.

As they walked on, Matilda said, "I thought of giving them a penny or so, but children need to wait for goodies at Christmas. Makes it more special."

"What do you want for Christmas, Leia?" Pilar asked.

"I want a new saddle and to ride Cinnamon all by myself."

Jane exchanged glances with Rose and Matilda. They already knew the surprise awaiting Leia. It would be both her birthday and special Christmas gift.

They spent the afternoon visiting one shop after another.

"Look at all those pastries," Rose said, pointing to the bakery window. "And the confectioners will have candy like you don't see any other time of the year."

Jane marveled at all the toys, dolls, fabric, jewelry, books, Bibles, and Christmas decorations representing many countries. Everyone was friendly and would even stop to introduce themselves instead of bustling around in a rush.

After the wonderful, fun-filled outing,

Rose took Jane aside and held her hands. "Jane, I want to thank you for what you're doing for my son and my granddaughter."

Jane started to protest, but Rose shook her head. "Don't be modest. You're exactly what Mak needed. No one else had been able to get through to him. The rest of us were just nagging. But you have made him think. Made him feel again. I think he's in the process of healing. Just . . . thank you."

She wrapped her arms around Jane, and they embraced. When Jane stood back, she could honestly say, "It's my pleasure."

The expression on Rose's face was warm. She smiled before walking away to the cart. Jane thought about what she'd just said. She'd never had the opportunity to give of herself like this before. Of course, she helped out, visiting the sick and taking food when there was a need. But this was different. Teaching Leia to ride and the difference between Little People and Jesus was a highlight of her life. That was such a wonderful opportunity God had given her. Also, being a friend to Mak. Yet she received so much from him. She could not imagine enjoying the island so much without him.

As she watched the cart disappear down the road, her aunt observed, "You're going to twist that finger right off one of these days."

Jane gave her a look. Maybe the finger, but the ring had to stay on it. Without it, as Matilda had emphasized, she would not be teaching a little girl to ride, or riding across the range and associating with that challenging man, her friend . . . Mak MacCauley.

CHAPTER 27

Mak stood on the crowded beach with the other islanders. Last year, he'd done his duty and brought his mother and Leia. He'd swooped Leia up onto his shoulders so she could see everything and get an early glimpse of Santa. His heart had not been in it.

Now, he stood without a member of his family, was not an active participant, but felt a part of it. He spoke to those near him and they commented on the festivities. He applauded with the others when the candles on the huge Christmas tree were lighted. The tree was adorned with garlands of colorful flowers.

A band of men began strumming their bragas. Schoolchildren were wearing white blouses with red and white skirts reminiscent of hula skirts. Red leis hung across their chests and down their backs, and red bands of leis circled their heads. They sang and signed the language with their graceful hands. Marching down the beach in front of the islanders, they sang Christmas songs. Pilar and Susanne walked side by side, singing.

Susanne's parents, his friends the Honeycutts, would be around somewhere. He hadn't kept up that friendship very well. Only now did he stop and think they had lost Maylea, too — as a friend.

Thinking of a friend, he felt a smile when the church adult choir, singing their hymns, came onto the beach. Pansy was conspicuously missing, but Jane, Matilda, and his mother were there. His mother had volunteered to sing with them this year, and she had been happier lately than he'd seen her in years.

They were followed by the children's choir, all wearing white dresses with the red leis and headbands that had been assembled in Rev. Russell's kitchen.

The choir director led everyone on the beach in singing "O Little Town of Bethlehem" and "Noel." After the sky turned from orange-red to gray, fireworks exploded like myriad multicolored stars over ships displaying flags in the harbor and the boats along the shore.

He wondered what Jane thought of all

that. That the stars and everything else in Texas were bigger and better? Texas couldn't be bigger than the ocean.

A canoe came into sight. Children began to yell and wave and crowd the shoreline. Santa arrived in his canoe, dressed in red. His flowing white hair and beard moved in the gentle night breeze as men wearing red leis rowed him to the shore. He stepped out with a big canvas bag from which he drew a gift for every child.

After Santa returned to the canoe, men bearing torches led the way to the church. Mak hesitated. He hadn't attended a service in so long — except for two funerals.

It was like he was seeing the church for the first time, although he'd grown up in it. His eyes wandered to the attendees, who crowded into the high-backed wooden pews and meshed together around the walls. A few stood at the doors and open windows, still able to see the church adorned with cypress branches, a Christmas tree with flowers and gifts, and candles of red and green. Rev. Russell delivered his message of Christmas, the birth of the world's Savior.

That was his pastor. Many of these people were his friends. His students sang. His mother and child sang their praises to God and the Savior. This was a world he hadn't allowed into his heart in more than three years.

After the final prayer, the torchbearers distributed red and green candles. The first one was lighted by a whale-oil lamp and then used to light another. The procedure was repeated throughout the congregation, representing their fellowship one with another.

He thought of the money the king had spent to illuminate his palace. His little girl, holding one little candle, was as important to God as the king.

He lit his own candle from another and passed the flame to the wick of another. One could go through the motions of living without really being alive.

Then the reverend was asking everyone to stand, and he began singing "Blest Be the Tie That Binds."

Mak needed to let Jane know just how much her friendship meant to him. Maybe he'd get the opportunity tomorrow when his new friends came for Christmas dinner.

Mak had not been so excited about Christmas since he was a child. No matter how festive a Christmas Eve, there was a church full of islanders for the Christmas Day service. Mak sat with his mother and Leia on the pew with Matilda and Jane. Leia sat very straight and kept smoothing her pretty new red dress his mother had given her that morning.

They would all go to his home after the service and have a feast Coco and his mother had been preparing for days. Maybe next year, he'd have a luau for all his workers, like his dad used to do. But for now this would do. Getting back into life was almost overwhelming for him.

The fabulous dinner and nice gifts were a treat for them all. Leia was completely happy with the new saddle she got for Cinnamon, and more than once, Mak saw her look at it and feel it, her eyes shining with the hope that she might finally be able to ride Cinnamon all by herself. She kept saying she wasn't afraid anymore.

"I think it's time for my present to you," Jane said.

Leia loved the stylish little riding suit to go with the boots Mac had bought for her, with Jane's help. She ran from the room and returned, turning and posing.

Jane described her perfectly. "You look like the world's greatest equestrienne, Leia."

Everyone applauded.

Mak picked up the saddle. "It's time."

He had her wait in the corral while he

brought out Cinnamon. He helped her up. Jane held the reins and walked them around the corral. "Now you do it," she said, "like I taught you."

Mak didn't expect what happened. He was not a crying man. But seeing Leia — his and Maylea's child, yet a person within herself — was overwhelming. He left the corral, and after composing himself, he came out with her surprise.

Fortunately, Jane had already taken Leia off Cinnamon, otherwise the child might have jumped off and broken her neck. She stood frozen, her hands on her face, her little lips forming a big *O,* and her eyes wide.

Mak led the snow-white pony into the corral and handed the reins to Leia. "Happy birthday," he said.

Her eyes roamed over the beautiful pony. "The pony is for me?" She pointed to her chest.

"Yes, she's yours."

"Ohhh." She dropped the reins and ran.

He thought she would run and maybe try to get on the pony, but she ran to him, threw her arms around him, and said, "Oh thank you, Daddy. Thank you. I love you so much. You must love me" — she spread her arms — "a whole bunch."

Had she doubted it?

"Okay, your pony's getting lonesome."

She stepped away and asked, "Can her name be Hoku?"

"Whatever you like," he said, "but why Star?"

"Because," she said as if he should know, "this is not a Little People story. Miss Jane said it's real. Jesus was a little baby. And a star was moving in the sky. A biiig one. And kings brought gold like Miss Tilda gives to everybody. He was important, and the kings kept looking at the star, and it helped them find the baby." She smiled broadly. "I'm important to you, and if I ever ride off like the wind like Miss Jane does and if I get lost, this Star will bring me back." She punctuated that with a nod.

"Sounds like a deal to me," he said. "But you know you have to get to know Hoku before you can ride her. You and she can grow up together."

"But I can ride Cinnamon." She pursed her lips. "I mean, when you and Miss Jane tell me."

"You're one smart little girl."

Smiling, she turned to pat the neck of Hoku firmly and speak softly to her.

Jane couldn't have asked for a better Christmas. She felt like she celebrated it in a way that Jesus would be pleased. She silently wished Him a happy birthday and thanked Him for the people she cared about and with whom she had spent Christmas Day.

When the others went out to the surrey, Mak said to Jane, "Just a moment."

With happy voices sounding outside, Mak looked down at her. "You've given so much to me and my family. How can I ever repay you?"

She didn't think he really expected an answer. It was simply a way to express his gratitude. Indirectly, she had a part in bringing father and daughter closer together. Seeing that was payment enough.

She could get all serious and tell him to stop trying to get revenge on a horse, to let go of his obsessive grief over Maylea. But that wouldn't be answering what he could do for her.

What could Mak give her?

Rather than get all serious after such a lovely day, she lifted her chin, gave him a challenging look, and said, "Show me something in Hawaii that I can never forget, something to take my breath away."

Immediately, he said, "A green sunset."

She laughed. "I've seen the unbelievably brilliant red and orange and golden sky at sunset. Is this green thing one of those Little

People stories?"

"It's for real. It's right as the sun dips into the ocean or vanishes into the horizon. There's a blue-green flash." Grinning, he said, "I would like to see the color of your eyes when that happens."

"Have you seen the green sunset?"

"Once," he said. "I was riding across the range on Big Brown, looking for a horse that had escaped from the corral. And it happened."

"Were you alone?"

His eyes looked puzzled. "Other men were nearby, also looking for the horse. But yes, I think you could say I was alone."

"You never saw the green sunset with . . . Maylea."

He seemed to study her for a moment before he answered. "No. She had seen it a few times in her life, but we didn't try to see it together."

She would really like to do something or see something that was his and hers alone, that he hadn't done with Maylea. "I think," she said, "that's what would take my breath away."

CHAPTER 28

Mak liked to give his paniolos and all the workers he could time off around Christmas and New Year, which meant more work for him. He didn't want Jane to spend her holiday teaching at the ranch. He thought it a good time for him to spend time with his little girl, and they even trotted along, he on Big Brown and she on Cinnamon outside the corral and on the range.

He and his daughter were bonding in a new and delightful way. They could talk about horses and ranches, and he realized she loved the ranch. He even talked to her about Maylea, and she smiled at his stories.

A week after Christmas, the invitation came from the king. The Royal Prerace Party would be held the third week in January. He and his mother were invited.

"Mak," his mother said, excitement coloring her voice, "even if you don't want to go, Matilda and I could."

Guilt washed over him like a tidal wave. He'd believed his mother over the past few years when she'd said she felt fine about not going, that she didn't want to leave Leia alone. And there had been the matter of the king purchasing that horse.

"Yes, Mother. Let's invite Matilda and Jane to accompany us."

"Oh." She rushed over, held his shoulders, and kissed his cheek. He had pleased his mother. He seemed to be doing a lot of that lately.

After that, it was like living in a different world. Jane continued to teach Leia horseback riding and how to take care of her pony. The women got together and talked about fashion and hairstyles.

As Mak shrugged into his dark waistcoat, trousers, and tailcoat, he wondered if the party would take Jane's breath away. Mak had seen the palace since the electricity had been installed, and it was still the talk of the island, but this party would be on the king's yacht. The king had many friends on Hawaii, but many of them found it too far to make a trip to Oahu. The king enjoyed having yacht parties, anyway.

Mac's mother stuck her head in the doorway of his bedroom as he tied the white bow tie at the neck of his winged-collar shirt.

She called him handsome, but she was biased.

"You look beautiful, Mother," he said when she walked into the room.

"Thank you. But I wonder how the queen will be dressed. Matilda said the latest style coming in Europe is dresses without bustles, if you can imagine that." She pointed her finger at him. "But I will not give up my corset."

"Well, I should think the bustles could go," he said. "Maybe they should put some of that material on the neckline."

"Oh, Mak," she chided. "This is the style. I don't want to look old-fashioned."

"Now haven't you women been trying on dresses for the past two weeks? And I'll bet Matilda knows more about the latest style than the princess. Regardless, you don't want to outdress the princess."

"I don't?" She patted her hair in an elaborate upsweep, decorated with jeweled combs. He had not seen her in formal dress since his dad had died. She had missed a lot, having lost her husband and taking care of Mak and Leia. He'd taken her for granted.

The clatter of horses' hooves and wheels outside sent his mother hurrying into the hallway. The next thing he knew, Leia,

Coco, Pilar, and Susanne were gushing over each other's attire. Mak had contacted Susanne's parents, and when he discovered they were going to the party, he had invited Susanne and Pilar to stay the night at his house.

Matilda was elaborately dressed in purple satin and wore jewels like a queen. "You're particularly stunning this afternoon," he said.

She thanked him graciously.

Jane came up to him. "And who is this handsome gentleman?" She straightened his white bow tie.

"I don't know anymore," he said. "This friend came along and —" He didn't need to get morbid, or gushy. "Your eyes are so blue." He liked the way she dressed. The look was elegant but less elaborate than the other ladies. Her hair was in an updo with little tendrils framing her forehead and the sides of her face. "I like your dress," he said.

"Thank you," she said, and soon they were in the surrey headed for the dock where they'd board the yacht that was waiting to take them away from civilization.

As they drew near, Matilda exclaimed, gazing at the gleaming white yacht larger than most ships, "My, that's a far cry from the ship we came over on."

"The king and princess try to copy Europe in every way they can," Rose said. "They do not want to be thought backward."

"This yacht," Mak explained, "was built in the United States. It was sold to the king for eighty thousand dollars' worth of sandalwood."

Rose nodded. "Our island is now almost bereft of sandalwood. It was in such demand in other places, and logging it provided a livelihood for islanders."

Matilda put her hand to her ear. "I hear music."

"The royal family are avid musicians," Rose explained. "They write songs, and the king has his own Royal Hawaiian Band."

"As soon as guests are aboard," Mak added, "the band will play, and we will sing 'Hawaii Ponoi,' written by the king. It's the Hawaiian national anthem. The royal family particularly likes the instrument called a braga or cavaquinho."

The dock was inundated with guests arriving by surreys and carriages. Some came in canoes and boats.

Royal horsemen were on hand to park the vehicles. Mak could feel the excitement. One didn't arrive late for the king's party.

Soon, guests were gathered on the deck, talking and greeting newcomers and others they'd known for many years. A nearby band strummed the bragas.

"We're moving out into the ocean," Jane said, leaning toward Mak to whisper. Her eyes shone with excitement.

"You don't have a yacht in Texas?" he teased.

She shook her head. "Not even a king."

"Ah," he said. "We finally have something bigger and better than Texas."

"No, no," she corrected him quickly. "We have oil, remember."

"I do," he said. "But our whales used to provide the world's oil supply before oil was discovered in Pennsylvania."

"Oh." She looked around. "Hawaii has disappeared."

"Yes," Mak said, "and about time for —"

The glass doors opened. A royal servant, looking stiff in his formal European clothes, announced, "King David Kalakaua and Queen Kapiolani."

The guests applauded.

The queen looked like a European monarch and wore her tiara. The king was dressed in his royal regalia, including his crown. They stood at attention as a band inside began to play the national anthem and the guests sang.

Jane looked up at Mak questioningly, but

he just smiled. She'd find out what was going on soon enough.

The king and queen turned and reentered the room. The servant announced each guest as they followed. The guests found places at tables while the king and queen stood somberly on a stage.

"Well," Matilda said. "Their clothing and way of announcing guests is how they do it in Europe."

Mak figured that meant she had visited such royalty.

"The king is quite handsome the way his beard seems like long sideburns fluffed out," Jane added.

"And that's a massive mustache, too," Matilda said. "How old is he?"

"Fifty-three," Rose said in a low tone. "He's been ill. But he looks fine tonight."

"The queen is beautiful," Jane added.

Mak agreed, but she did not outshine these ladies at his table. As soon as the guests were inside, the king's face became all smiles, and his eyes danced. He removed his royal coat. His shirt was exquisite, but he could pass as simply a well-dressed man. "Now," he said, "we dispense with this formality. Let the fun begin."

Other men took off their formal coats. Some, like Mak, rolled up their sleeves and removed their ties.

"There's food," the king said.

At that, sliding-glass doors opened.

"My," Matilda exclaimed. "That aroma is enough to tempt the whales."

"I don't think there are any," Jane said. "They've all been used up to make oil for the lamps here in Hawaii."

Mak shook his head.

"And we drink," the king said, "including Hawaii's famous Kona coffee." Servants in black pants, flowered shirts, and red vests lined up inside the doors, waiting to ensure the guests were properly served their dinner.

"And be merry," he shouted.

"He is known as the merry king," Mak said as the lively music began, and the king grabbed his queen, and they began to dance.

Others joined them, while some went into the side room for food and drink.

After that dance, young men and women ran in from a side room and onto the stage.

"They may try to copy the Europeans," Matilda said, "but that is not ballroom dancing."

On stage, the hula dancers were swaying and moving their graceful hands while a man crooned a song. When they finished, the hula dancers came to the guests, taking several on stage. His three ladies were selected. Matilda was a riot. His mother had talents he'd been unaware of, and Jane was adorable.

When the guests returned, the dancers kept Matilda on stage to demonstrate dances from Europe and some Texas square-dance steps. Mak looked beyond the glass doors. "Looks like the sun is getting ready to set. Shall we?"

CHAPTER 29

"This is a wonderful party," Jane said as Mak led her outdoors and around to the back of the deck where the music and voices sounded faintly in the background. The sky had turned Jane into gold, and he smiled, remembering Leia saying, "Gold like Miss Matilda gives everybody."

Miss Matilda couldn't give this strong-willed young woman to anybody.

He leaned over, his arms against the railing. Jane stood holding on with her hands. She looked over at him. "You seemed to be having a good time. During the hula, were you thinking of Maylea?"

He straightened. "Yes and no," he said honestly. "Of course she was in my memory. But thanks to you, I was thinking of . . . you . . . the fun . . . your having a good time. Sometimes with you, my friend, I am in the moment. Thank you for that."

She turned toward him about to say

something, but he caught hold of her arm. "The sky is magenta, without any clouds. Everything is right for the green flash."

Jane shifted her gaze to the sun.

"No, don't stare at the sun. That's not good for the eyes. Look away until only the very top of the sun is about to disappear into the ocean."

"Okay."

He saw her shoulders and chest rise with her accelerated breathing, anticipating as she stared at him, glanced at the sun, and at him. She whispered. "It's almost there."

"Now," he said. "Look at it and don't blink."

She squealed. "Ah! I did. I saw it." She grabbed his arms, looked up into his face and back at the horizon. "I really did. It was only a moment. All the greens of Hawaii are different from any I have ever seen. This was even greener. And even more beautiful. I don't know how to explain it."

"Nobody does," he said, looking into her delighted, lovely face.

Then her lips parted. An ethereal expression bathed her face. "There's a rainbow. Am I crazy, or is that a rainbow?"

"Of course it's a rainbow. It always happens after the green flash. You see, a rainbow is created when a raindrop —"

"No," she said, "Don't explain it. Just let me bask in it."

As she basked, their faces were so close. Neither was looking at the rainbow. He felt her warm breath tantalizing his lips. She seemed to lean forward. It must have been him. But her face lifted to his.

As if they had a mind of their own, his lips met her soft warm ones, and he felt lost in the moment until finally it was as if he were saying to himself what he had to say to Panai so often: Hold on, hold back, you mustn't give it your all, be controlled.

Where the will came from he didn't know, but somehow he stepped back and grasped the railing, feeling as panicked as if a tsunami was upon him.

What could he do? Run? Jump in the ocean? What was she doing? He was afraid to look. "I'm sorry. Forgive me."

"No, it's all right."

"I have no right. I've ruined everything. I don't know why —"

"Mak, it's because we're a man and a woman."

He exhaled heavily and managed to look at her. She was facing him. "But you're engaged," he protested, "and I'm as together as a shipwreck."

She gave a weak smile. "But you're not

engaged, Mak. So I'm more to blame if we're going to place blame. After I saw the green flash and the rainbow, I just had to do something. So I closed my eyes and —"

"You closed your eyes?"

"Well I had to blink, didn't I?"

"Of course." He took a deep breath. "Jane, I know you're trying to make light of this —"

Before he could finish, her fingers touched his lips. They were soft as her voice. "Friends can kiss." She kissed his cheek.

She was trying to make it sound so innocent. "Your fiancé might not think so."

"Austin would understand. It was . . . a moment. Not something bad or evil."

"No," he said. "It was —" He shrugged. "Human?"

He nodded. "Very human." He paced. "I'm supposed to be the more mature, older, been married —"

"I know, Mak, that you feel guilty. Your whole life is wrapped up in guilt and anger. This was only . . ." She smiled. "A lovely moment."

He looked down. Was that all?

"We are both single, you know."

Yes, he was making too much of it. But single? Was he? No. He was married to his guilt and grief.

"Did you see the green sunset?" she asked.

Staring at her, his hand touched her arm. "I saw the blue green flash in your eyes."

"Oh, so here you are," came Matilda's voice as the sky darkened to a dull gray. "I just finished dancing with the king. Wheee! They'd have me dancing all night if I would. It's social time now, but I thought I needed a little reprieve."

"Excuse me," Mak said. "I want to speak to some friends I haven't seen in a while."

Jane turned and leaned against the railing. "You saw?"

"Yes dear. I was fascinated by the idea I might see a green sunset. Too bad I didn't bring a gentleman friend with me."

"Matilda!"

"Sorry dear. I'm just doing what you did. Trying to make light of it."

"Shocked?"

"Me? Oh honey. Not even surprised. He has become your goal, your purpose. He needs you, and you responded to that. Austin never needed you that way. Mak has touched your heart in a different way. You're growing up."

"Austin would never hurt me," Jane said. "Mak . . . could."

Matilda stood so close their shoulders

touched. "You say you love Austin." Jane nodded. "And that you and Mak are just friends. Do I have that right?"

"Yes, I claim that."

"Pray about what is right, Jane."

"Okay. But I'm not sure Mak prays anymore. Maybe what's right for me isn't right for him."

"Everything here is new and different. You've been rather sheltered in Texas. You're trying your wings. When the time is right, all those befuddled questions will . . ." She gestured out over the ocean. "They'll float away. Shall we join the others?"

Jane nodded. "I'll be right there."

She stood looking out over the deep blue water. Austin was out there, heading her way. The stars in the sky winked like they were playing some kind of trick on her.

Lifting her chin, she straightened her shoulders and turned to walk back to the royal party.

She'd seen her green sunset.

But that wasn't what took her breath away.

CHAPTER 30

In mid-January, everything changed. Leia was allowed to start attending school, in part because Rose took Mak's teaching spot. Matilda offered to assist. The two women loved the arrangement.

Two afternoons after school each week, Jane continued her lessons with Leia. Mak spent most of his time making sure Panai was ready for the big race. On the days she didn't see him at the stables, she rode out to the racetrack.

Sometimes he was there. He didn't seem to mind her presence, but his mind obviously was on the horse. One day when Mak wasn't there, Chico brought Panai over to the fence and dismounted.

He barely spoke to Jane and looked distressed. "Be back in a minute, Tomas."

"Your stomach again?" Tomas said.

Chico ran into the stable. Tomas looked worried. "He's been getting that lately," he confided to Jane. "Seems to be getting worse."

Chico soon returned. "I feel better now," he said, but his brown skin looked pasty.

"You're in no condition —" Tomas began.

"I have no choice, Tomas. You know that."

There was only one thing a well-meaning girl could do. Not that she wanted Chico to be sick, but her heartbeat accelerated at what she was thinking. "Let me ride him," Jane said.

The two men looked at her like she was *loco.*

"No way," Chico said at the same time Tomas said, "Never happen."

"Why not?"

Chico looked like a little color had returned to his face. "Nobody rides Panai but me and the boss."

"I rode Panai with the boss, remember?"

"But that was a pleasure ride. He didn't take the horse for all he was worth."

"Let me be your substitute. I'll give Panai a good workout."

As if Panai understood, he stepped up and nuzzled the side of Jane's face with his soft nose. She turned, laughed, and patted the lucky white spot on his face. "See, he loves me."

Chico seemed to hold his breath.

Tomas glared at him. "You'll have to fight me to get on that horse, Chico."

"Tomas, my health means nothing if I don't win this race for Mr. Mak. You know that's what will bring back to us the man he used to be."

"And what was that?" Jane said.

Tomas looked away as Chico said, "Not depressed, I guess. He's not been right for three years. Just as I can tell when a horse likes a person, I can tell when a man likes a woman. Mr. Mak likes you, Miss Jane. If you were not wearing that ring, you maybe could help him get back his sanity."

"Thank you, Chico." But if she wasn't wearing that ring, she wouldn't be there.

Chico grabbed his stomach, then let out a ragged breath. "Just one time around. Slow." He paused, looking doubtful. "He may not even let you get on him."

"Of course he will," she said to Panai, who seemed to nod in agreement. "We understand each other."

He nodded. "I've heard you teaching Miss Leia. You know horses."

Jane thought that was a pretty good compliment coming from a jockey who would race a horse against the king's horse.

"Please let me help," Jane said. "Mak trusts me with his daughter. Surely a horse

233

isn't more important than his daughter."

Both men stared at her as if they weren't sure about that. Neither was she.

"Chico, give me a few pointers on how a jockey sits and leans into the horse."

He did, and when he said, "You have to control him, hold him back," she knew he was consenting and began climbing the fence.

"You can't let him go at top speed. He wants to, but he has to save that for the race. He'll understand when he gets on that racetrack. But for now, he has to hold back."

Jane remembered Mak leaning into her and telling Panai that exact thing. She could do it.

Like Mak had guided Panai the day she rode with them, she started him at a trot, then picked up speed. She could tell he wanted to go, but he yielded to her control. If she gave the signal, or he decided to, he could jump that fence and they'd fly away like a bird.

Now there was no Mak to distract her. As much as she wanted to give full rein, she held Panai — and herself — back. Nevertheless, although she thought she'd ridden like the wind before, now she knew she had not. Panai took her for the ride of her life, as if she had wings.

As they neared Tomas and Chico, she didn't want to stop. But she had to obey the rules.

Tomas and Chico complimented her profusely. There was only one thing she could say. "That was almost as exhilarating as a green sunset . . . almost."

CHAPTER 31

Mid-February arrived. So did Austin, Buck Buckley, and Inez Ashcroft. The bells rang, and the islanders turned out to watch the liner come in. Mak knew he had to be there. These American visitors were relatives and friends of . . . his new friends. To stay away would be the height of impropriety.

So he stood back as he had done when Jane, Matilda, and Pilar had arrived. He held his hat in his hand and observed as his mother and Leia, along with his new friends and Reverend Russell gave leis and hugs and kisses.

Jane and Austin's kiss was brief. But they were in public.

He mustn't stand aside as if not a part of the group, so he stepped up and held out his hand to be introduced. Miz Ashcroft was a fine-looking woman. The men would be tremendously impressive to the islanders, who never got their fill of what, or who, a ship might bring in. They would not be disappointed by these men, fine specimens of what cultured westerners should look like.

Mak felt rather like a rugged paniolo in comparison. On second thought, he supposed that's what he was.

Then Jane was telling her father that Mak's ranch was even bigger than his.

Her daddy almost roared. "I didn't know they made ranches any bigger than what's in Texas." He pointed at Mak. "This I gotta see to believe, son."

"Will be my pleasure." Despite his dignified appearance, Mr. Buckley, who said to call him "Buck," smiled broadly, and Mak liked what he believed was genuine friendliness.

"And this," Jane said, "is my . . . Austin."

Was she going to say my fiancé? Or was she saying "my Austin" for emphasis? It didn't really matter. Mak shook the hand of the well-dressed, nice-looking, tall, friendly man. Like looking at a horse, you could tell when it was well-bred.

Mak said what he needed to say to friends of his friends. "Jane, I know you'll want to show Austin the island. I'll handle Leia's lessons. Next week if it's convenient, come out to the ranch for dinner, and I'll show everyone the ranch."

"Yes," his mother said. "Buck and you, Inez. And of course" — she gestured around — "all of you."

A week later when Mak's mother and daughter returned from school, his mother said Jane wanted to come the following afternoon for Leia's lesson. Austin would come with her, and Mak might want to show him the ranch.

Just as Mak was thinking they probably weren't interested in accepting his polite dinner invitation, his mother added, "They are looking forward to having dinner with us, Mak. And Buck is anxious to see the ranch. Right now, they're getting Inez settled in Pilar's bedroom. Buck and Austin are staying in a hotel in town."

"They could have stayed here."

Her eyebrows lifted. "You didn't ask them to."

When Austin and Jane rode up, Mak realized he hadn't asked Austin if he would like to take one of his horses while on the island. But one couldn't think of everything upon first meeting. Austin wore a smart-looking riding outfit and rode on a fine-looking horse he must have rented in town.

He and Jane looked . . . good together.

Leia came out in her riding outfit, ready for her lesson. Austin said he'd heard she was a very good rider and had a pony named Star. "Texas is called the Lone Star State," he said.

Mak remembered he and Jane had talked about that and laughed together.

Leia looked up at him. "I don't ever want Miss Jane to leave. Are you going to take her away?"

After a quick glance at Jane, he knelt in front of Leia, getting down to her size. "Well, from what I've seen of Hawaii this week and from what I've heard, it seems that many people who come here never want to leave."

Leia seemed to take that as fact. She smiled and took Jane's hand in hers. They headed for the corral.

As the two men rode out on the range, Mak noted that Austin sat in the saddle like one accustomed to good riding habits. He wondered if Austin was really interested in seeing a ranch. But what else did he have to show him? Then it occurred to him. He could show friendship.

Before he could ask Austin about the oil business, however, Austin said, "Mak, Jane told me about your wife. I'm sorry about that."

That was nice of him, and Mak acknowledged it with a nod. "Have you ever lost anyone close?" he asked.

"Not immediate family," he said. "I've been blessed."

Mak wondered how Austin would feel if he lost a wife . . . or a loved one. He wouldn't wish that on anyone.

"From what Jane's said about you, Austin, I get the impression you've never loved anyone but her." He was surprised when Austin hesitated.

Austin looked out over the range and the corral as they approached it. Finally, he said, "To be honest with you, Mak, I've had my years of indiscretion, sorry to say. During college, but they were passing fancies."

Mak said what was on his mind. "I'm surprised you waited so long to marry her."

"So am I, in a way," Austin said. "After my college years, I was ready to make that lifetime commitment. She wasn't. She was smarter than I in knowing she wasn't ready. I was willing to wait and threw myself into the business."

Mak thought Austin had a good outlook on things. He was surprised that he talked so openly about his and Jane's relationship. But then Austin was talking about someone he had a future with. Mak didn't have a future with Maylea.

"I've given this a lot of thought in the past few months," Austin went on, "being thousands of miles from Jane, with her completely out of reach. I knew when she said she would come to Hawaii it would be a milestone. She'd told me she would be ready to settle down after this trip." Austin was nodding. "I was right. She's different."

That surprised Mak. "Different?"

Austin nodded. "Different than when she was in Texas. She's matured. She's found purpose in teaching your daughter and in being your friend along with relating to her uncle Russell."

"She's changed my life." Mak felt warm under Austin's scrutiny.

"Mak, I don't think Jane knows she's changed your life."

"Well I haven't changed a lot of my actions or my attitudes, so it doesn't show."

"The changes in Jane show. I now know that at eighteen, she couldn't be the mature woman I wanted." He smiled over at Mak. "She's matured a lot since being here. Her goal is no longer winning the top spot in equestrienne events."

"What?"

Austin laughed lightly. "She's always been second. Absolutely couldn't stand it to think anyone would beat her in any competition."

"I figured she was first," Mak said.

Austin shook his head. "Second."

Mak was trying to absorb why the conversation was going this way. Was Austin warning him not to take Jane's relating to him personally because she found purpose in it? Was he saying don't bother letting Jane know she changed your life because she'd never accept being second place, or rather second wife, in a man's life? Had Jane told Austin about the green-sunset *friendly* kiss?

Mak drew a deep breath. He started to say maybe they shouldn't be talking about her. But Austin said he and Jane had talked about him. Austin and Jane had talked about Mak. What should a man in love talk about — coconut palms?

They rode up to the racetrack and dismounted to watch Chico give Panai his workout. He could tell Austin appreciated the horse, but not in the way he and Jane did. Then again, Austin wasn't a horseman; he was an oil man.

Mak mentioned they might go back to the house, but Austin expressed the desire to ride farther. "Jane mentioned the sugar fields."

"Yes, we'll ride out that way," he said, glad Austin wasn't bored.

"Mak," Austin said, as they rode across the velvety green range. "You asked if I lost anyone. I've heard about your situation. So I'm going to be honest with you."

Which situation? came instantly to Mak's mind. Then he reminded himself there was only one situation, and that was the loss of his wife and his getting revenge on that horse because of it.

"I haven't lost a person," Austin said, "but when I was abroad studying in England, away from authority, from prying eyes, I lost my way for a while. I lost my relationship with God through philandering. I didn't even think of it that way at the time. My letters home were the same. My feelings for Jane and family were the same. But the — I guess you call it the baser side — surfaced. At the time I called it fun, just young people having fun."

Mak nodded. "I suppose many of us can identify with that, Austin."

Austin agreed. "But after graduation, I realized how foolish I'd been, how I'd disappointed God. I felt like a worm. By the way," he said, looking over at Mak. "I didn't tell Jane about that. I had to find myself, to identify with God. There comes a defining moment when . . ."

Mak's mind wandered. A moment . . . a

kiss . . . a green sunset. But what was Austin saying? A moment when a person as an adult decided to live for the Lord, no matter what. No longer straddle the fence.

"I felt Jane would find that in this trip, and she has."

Mak realized Austin was describing a spiritually defining moment. He'd never thought of things in quite that way. If he tried to identify a defining moment, it would be when he decided to marry Maylea, be a husband, a dad, a man.

But was that a commitment to a woman, to a lifestyle . . . and not to God? To love and serve Him, regardless? No, he had not had a spiritually defining moment as an adult.

Maybe after Panai won the race, he would think on these things. Everything would have changed then. He would have had his revenge. Jane, Austin, and the others would leave Hawaii. Leia would again be without a mother figure except the one who should only be a grandmother.

"Thank you, Austin, for your honest words." A short ironic laugh came from his throat. "I wouldn't be able to talk with you or even listen to anything personal, anything spiritual, had Jane not laid the groundwork."

"Maybe that's because we're visitors to

the island, Mak. We won't be around to remind you of your having spoken your heart."

They came to the fence and stopped the horses. "That's sugar cane," he said, and they gazed out on the acres of slender green leaves swaying in the gentle breeze.

Mak knew Jane was the one who had encouraged him to speak his heart. "Austin, I don't think I spoke personally because you're a visitor who will leave. I wouldn't mind if you were a permanent resident. I think we could be friends."

Austin nodded. "I think we are. Who knows? Jane might decide she doesn't want to leave. This is a special place. I can understand why it's called paradise."

Mak liked having a friend, speaking his heart to a man. Most men didn't do that. Austin was, as Jane had implied, a special kind of man. Like Rev. Russell in some ways. Yes, it would be nice to have a male friend. But things with Jane would be different. They should not have kissed; she should not have seen the green sunset.

His heart was troubled. Without being obvious, he turned his head far enough to see Austin's expression.

The man looked at peace. There was a warmth in his eyes, a strength in his being.

Probably that came from loving and being loved by a wonderful woman with whom he planned to spend his life. Yet Austin had attributed his confidence to a relationship with God.

CHAPTER 32

"Daddy," Jane said, "is there something between you and Inez that I need to know about?"

"Nothing I can talk about until after I have my beautiful daughter married off and settled. Now, how long you gonna keep me waitin', girl?"

"You don't have to wait for me, Daddy."

"But I will. I'm not about to have some old maid spinster around tying me down." He laughed and drew her into his arms.

Later, Uncle Russell was showing the school, church, and town to the others. Jane and Matilda sat at the table, drinking Kona coffee and talked about how Inez had taken on the airs of a demure southern lady, widow of the once-prominent Mr. Ashcroft, and worthy of the likes of Mr. John Buckley.

Jane thought she was.

"Do you think she would consider letting Pilar stay in Hawaii?"

"Pilar is making a good argument for it. She has plans to attend that nursing school along with Susanne. Inez was impressed by that."

Jane sighed. "I know how Pilar feels. I would love to stay in Hawaii for a long time. Austin mentioned having a second home here."

Matilda gave her a long look. "Isn't that supposed to make you happy?"

"Well, it would really be three homes. One of them would be the long voyages from Hawaii to America and back again. And those ships are not yachts."

"My dear Jane," Matilda said resolutely. "When you're in love, you don't care if it's Texas, Hawaii, the middle of the ocean, or the swamps in Florida. You just want to be with the one you love."

Jane brought her hand down on the table. "Of course it makes a difference."

Matilda wasn't rattled by her reaction. "Certainly you can prefer some places over another. But you wouldn't choose a place over the one you love."

Jane took a deep breath. "I think you're trying to tell me something."

"I don't think I have to tell you. You've known since you were eighteen years old and began to postpone marriage plans."

"I've always had reasons."

"I know," Matilda agreed. "No one ever marries if there's a death, an accident, a tornado, college." Matilda smiled — one of those caring, I-know-what-you-feel smiles that made Jane want to cry.

Jane knew she might as well say it. They both knew it anyway. "You said a place doesn't matter that much. I think the opposite can be true, too. No matter how much you love a place, it can lose its allure if you're not with the one you love."

Matilda nodded. "I've returned to some of the places my husband and I visited together. And you're right. It's not the same. It reminds me of that verse in the Bible. It must be in Proverbs. I can't imagine anyone else saying it, unless it's Solomon in Ecclesiastes. Anyway, it's something like it being better to live in a corner of a housetop than with a brawling woman in a wide house."

Jane gasped. "Matilda. I'm trying to get some advice from you, and you're changing this all around. Sounds to me like you're saying that's what Austin's life would be like if I married him."

"Well, it could very well be. My motherly advice is you must think of him, too. What kind of favor would you be doing him if you don't love him?"

"But I do love him. Of course I love him."

"I know, dear. But there are many kinds and degrees of love. You need to have a few butterflies in your tummy and hear the bells ring."

The bells had been ringing all day, every hour on the hour, reminding everyone of the race tomorrow, Hawaii's biggest event of the year. Mak felt sick. For him it wasn't just a race. It was his life. He'd been preparing himself and Panai for three years.

That night, unable to sleep, he walked out into the night several times, feeling like the edge of darkness was within.

He wouldn't go to the stables and check on Panai, lest he awaken Chico. His jockey needed to sleep. He kept telling himself that Panai was in perfect condition to win. He couldn't even pray about it. How could he ask God to help him get revenge on a horse?

He had arranged for Inez, Jane, and Austin to ride in Mak's surrey driven by Mr. Buckley. Rev. Russell would take his mother, Leia, Pilar, and Matilda.

Mak needed to go alone. He would need that regardless of the outcome, but particularly if his horse lost. But when he arrived and went to the holding area, they were all there — his friends and well-wishers.

"I'd like to quote a verse and pray," Rev. Russell said. "It's from Philippians. It goes something like this. 'This one thing I do, forgetting those things which are behind, and reaching forth unto those things which are before. I press toward the mark for the prize.' "

Then he prayed. Not for Mak's horse to win, but that it might be a good race for all concerned. Good clean entertainment. And for the Lord's will to be done in everything. He prayed for Chico.

Chico?

Mak didn't know if the reverend said *Amen* or not, but he almost shouted, "Where's Chico?" The loudspeaker was saying they should take their places. The others looked around.

"He'll probably be here any minute," Rev. Russell said.

"He should be here now." Mak took off running toward the stables.

CHAPTER 33

Tomas was standing over Chico, who lay on the straw, curled up in a corner. His breath was ragged, his eyes squinted, and his face drenched with sweat.

"What's going on?" Mak demanded.

"He needs a doctor."

Mak motioned for a stable boy. "Son, run get a doctor."

"No," Chico got to his feet. "I'll be all right." His jaw was clenched, and Mak knew he was fighting pain . . . and losing.

A doctor rushed in from one of the ambulances always on hand at a race. He ordered them to move back. Tomas mentioned previous attacks. The doctor said, "It may be appendicitis."

"Take his clothes off."

Recognizing the voice, Mak turned and stared hard at Jane. The others stood around her, staring, too, as if she'd lost her mind.

"I'll ride Panai."

His laugh was short. "That doesn't even deserve an answer."

"Please. I can do it."

"Mak," Austin said, and for an instant, Mak thought he might have an ally. Instead, Austin affirmed, "If she says she can ride him, she can."

Chico grunted as the doctor poked around his stomach. Between his gasps, he said, "Somebody has to, Mak. You know that. She may not be able to win, but she can ride him."

Tomas confirmed that with a nod. "He's right."

And how would they know? He didn't need to ask. Their sheepish looks told him they'd gone behind his back and let her ride alone. Realizing his hands were now fists, he unclasped them.

Why should he be so concerned about keeping Jane safe, when neither she nor those who claimed to love her, including her fiancé, didn't? With a lift of his hands and a snort like a disgruntled horse, he stomped out.

He'd probably have ridden off if Leia hadn't run after him and taken his hand. She looked up at him with pleading eyes. Her little lips trembled. "Daddy, Jesus will take care of Miss Jane. And Chico."

Mak didn't think he could stand it if God didn't take care of them. And what would that do to his little girl, to a faith that had begun in her? Not long ago, she would have credited the Little People.

He led Leia to the seats reserved for racehorse owners. The others filed in behind him. Leia sat on one side of him and Austin on the other. A glance around revealed a full stadium and spectators crowded around the edges.

Mak felt like he had sea legs when he stood with the others for the singing of the national anthem. He didn't attempt to join in.

After they were seated, the announcements began, followed by cheering. When he announced the black stallion Panai, son of the king's horse Akim, ridden by a substitute jockey, Miss Jane Marie Buckley, Mak was shocked. Amid the applause and shouting, both Austin and Matilda stood and whistled through their teeth.

Leia looked and stuck her fingers in her mouth, but the sound came out as *"Ffffff ffffff."*

He couldn't begin to cheer at a time like this. It could be dangerous for the best of jockeys. His gaze scanned the riders. They looked like what they were — winning jockeys. Jane sat erect in Chico's jockey suit, looking like an equestrienne who might have her horse jump over a two-foot hurdle.

As soon as the race started, he leaned over and held his face in his hands.

"Maybe I can catch a sunbeam and get this to shine in the eyes of the other horses," Austin said.

Mak looked as Austin brought the ring out of his pocket. That was a good idea. Take off the rock. It would certainly decrease the weight. "Aren't you afraid of what could happen?"

"Mak, I can't control what happens." Then he shoved the ring into his pocket. "I'll be praying and cheering."

Mak shook his head. "I don't care about winning. I only care about her safety." He gazed at the racetrack. It was no surprise that Akim was ahead from the beginning. Panai was midway. He stayed midway even when some horses passed him. He then passed another and eased to the outside.

Panai was easing on up. Mak knew his horse. A horse like Panai made racing look easy, and so could a jockey like Chico. Jane was doing well, even holding Panai back the way he'd done the day he let her ride with him.

Those around Mak were standing and

cheering and yelling. "Come on, Jane! Come on, Jane!"

It dawned on him that nobody cheered for a jockey. They cheered for a horse, and usually one they'd bet on.

Austin said, "Look, she's inching up."

Mak got to his feet. He couldn't yell. He heard his own pitiful whisper, "Jane."

They were nose and nose, and the finish line was right ahead. Mother and son. Would one give in to the other? No, they were champions. The one who killed his wife. And the one who would have the revenge.

The crowd went wild.

He couldn't tell which horse crossed the finish line first.

The announcer declared Panai the winner.

Mak sat down, put his hands over his face, and closed his eyes. This was the race that was to take away his grief and misery. Then why did he feel the way he did?

Austin sat down. "Hey, Mak. Did you see the finish?"

"Are they all right?"

"Look."

Mak looked. Jane and Panai were in the winner's circle. The announcement was still coming over the speaker. The princess was presenting her with the award. The king came from across the aisle, shook Mak's hand, and congratulated him.

"Shouldn't we go down?" Austin asked.

"You go congratulate her," Mak said.

"Not without you. It's your horse and your jockey. And your Big Island Cup."

Yes, Mak thought. *And your fiancée.*

CHAPTER 34

Jane watched Mak come into the winner's circle, heard his name announced and the applause that followed. He came over to Panai while photos were being taken. Lifting his head slightly, he nodded toward Jane, as if in thanks. He stared at the camera but made no attempt to smile.

After the photos, he accepted congratulations with handshakes. He thanked everyone, then said he would go to the hospital and see about Chico. He would see them all later.

Maybe he wasn't angry with her for riding, but he didn't appear pleased about the win. Perhaps he was just concerned about Chico. Her displeasure with him turned to guilt when she realized she had not thought of Chico from the time she dressed in that jockey suit and began the ride of her life . . . again.

"Did I do wrong?" she asked her companions as they left the racetrack.

In unison, they answered no.

"You and Panai won the most important race of the island. And you did it against the king's horse," Rose said. "That's what Mak has wanted for more than three years."

Regardless of whether Mak was angry with her for riding Panai, he wasn't thinking only of himself — he was concerned about Chico.

Much later, after returning home, bathing, and getting into comfortable clothes, Jane asked Austin if they could walk outside. They ambled out into the cool evening and went to the schoolyard, where Jane sat in a swing.

"Aren't you exhausted, Jane?"

"I think I'm still excited," she said. "But my emotions are so mixed. I'm elated, yet worried about Chico. I'm happy for Mak, but I'm not sure he is."

"Jane," Austin said, standing in front of her. "Let's talk about . . . us."

He took the diamond ring from his vest pocket. Jane looked down at her lap, where her right hand was folded over the left. She didn't raise it. Neither did he.

The night breeze whispered in the coconut palms. The rope swing was still, but her heart was doing an unfamiliar dance. When she looked up at Austin's disturbed expression, he said, "I have a confession to make."

Jane waited.

"You know Rebecca," he said.

"Rebecca?" Jane said. Rebecca. The one who got first place in equestrienne events. The twenty-four-year-old blond daughter of the president of Austin's company. The girl who could never return to her carriage without Austin accompanying her. The one whose blue eyes seemed to turn green with envy when she saw Jane and Austin together. The one Jane didn't want to get Austin — the top prize.

A sense of possessiveness rose in Jane, but if Austin confessed something, should she? This inner sense of honesty was getting to be a nuisance. "You wouldn't be talking about the person you and I have discussed for the past few years, would you?"

Austin shook his head as he had other times when they simply let the subject of Rebecca go by the wayside. He stared into her eyes. "She said you don't want to marry me; you just don't want to let me go. That I deserved better than being strung along for years."

It flashed through Jane's mind that Matilda had said something similar. More than once. "Do you feel strung along, Austin?"

"Maybe . . . kept waiting. But I wanted you to be sure. I'd never thought of it quite the way Rebecca said it." He paused, then blurted out, "She kissed me."

It looked like the two of them might be in the same boat. She couldn't help the ironic laugh that escaped her throat. "You kissed her back. I mean her lips?"

He scoffed. "Jane, how can you sit there and act like this is some child's prank? This amounts to disrespect for you. I've struggled with this. And about telling you." He paused. "Don't you care?"

"Well, yes. Describe it."

"Describe what?"

"The kiss."

His poor Adam's apple seemed to be getting a lot of exercise. "She is . . . was . . . very passionate."

"Were you?"

He took a step away and gazed at the ground. "I . . . surprised myself."

She could hardly believe it. "You were passionate?"

"Well, I was . . . tempted. Although I never told you details, I was honest about not living the way the Lord intended during my college years. But I've tried to since recommitting myself to the Lord. That's why I have to tell you this. I — I did return the kiss, but then I broke away and I turned and marched right out of the office."

"You left her standing there?"

"Yes, but she ran after me and made me talk. Or rather, listen."

"What did she say?"

"She said that she and I were made for each other. That she'd been in love with me for years. She thought I should know it. She said that your leaving for Hawaii made her decide to speak up. She thinks you don't love me the way she does."

Jane stood from the swing, still holding onto the rope. She wasn't really surprised, yet she felt jealous. She and Rebecca had been rivals since school days. She supposed that challenged them both to be their best. But this was not a game. Where was this leading?

Austin looked at the diamond ring he still held. He looked at Jane with a troubled expression. "Well," he said. "Do you? Love me that way? You've never . . . kissed me."

"What? Austin! I've kissed you all my life."

"I mean not like that. With your heart in it."

"Oh. You mean . . . that passionately."

His face tilted slightly, and the lift of his eyebrows indicated that was it.

"Well, we weren't supposed to."

"Rebecca and I weren't supposed to, either."

She nodded.

"Jane. I don't want some momentary indiscretion of mine to get in the way of what you and I mean to each other. But are you sure that you and I belong together . . . forever?"

She took a deep breath. All this needed to be faced, to be talked about, because what she had thought, she now said. "Austin, all of my life, I've believed that you and I were part of each other. Our families, even after my mother died, were like one family. I've always believed we were best friends, were going to be married, and live happily ever after."

"It's a beautiful dream," he said. "But I think you may have a different one now."

She grasped the rope tightly.

"Today, you risked your life for that man. You love his child. They're in your heart."

"So are you, Austin. You've always been there. You always will be. You've been my dearest friend."

"Yes," Austin said. "I made this trip because I knew we had to get this settled once and for all. Seeing that race, you on that horse, it was like seeing you as you really are for the first time. Riding toward another goal, away from me." He looked at the ring. "Mak is your equal, not I."

"He doesn't want me."

A wan smile touched Austin's lips. "That's for him to say." He returned the ring to his pocket, and Jane didn't know if she could stand it. "Oh Austin. You're wonderful. I've loved you as long as I can remember." She rushed to him.

He lifted a hand to still her words. "I didn't say he's better than I. Just your equal in many ways."

"You and I could have made a good life together."

"Yes, I think we could have."

Could have. Those words changed the thinking of a lifetime. With eyes that blurred, she fell against his chest. He held her tight. The sound coming from him sounded like the kind of sobs she felt in her own throat.

"I do love you, Jane," he said, when they could let go.

She took the handkerchief he offered. "I've always loved you. Always will."

Strange. This felt like . . . salt in a wound. It hurt. But it would heal.

Like the night, a calm seemed to settle over them.

"Jane, on the voyage over, I had a lot of time to think. I wonder. Maybe we've been more like a very close brother and sister."

She was shaking her head. "No. More like cousins."

He laughed, tears again forming in his eyes. "Kissing cousins."

She nodded. "But not . . . passionately enough."

He took his handkerchief from her and wiped her tears away, then swiped at his own. "You don't have to tell me, but I wonder. Do you know what it means to kiss someone passionately?"

She thought of the teenage kiss she had given the boy behind the barn. That was as passionate as she could get at the time. She thought of the nearness of Mak, his face, his lips, just his nearness that sped up her heartbeat and made her long to be in his arms. "In my dreams and in my weak moments, yes, Austin. I do. I haven't experienced it like you and Rebecca, but yes. I know."

He took a deep breath. "I thought so."

CHAPTER 35

After Mak walked away from his family and friends, he went to the area where the king and others stood with Akim. The king shook his hand. "Congratulations, Mak. I can imagine what this means to you. And if Akim had to be beaten, I'm glad it was by Panai."

The king held his hand a moment longer than necessary, with a strong grip as his gaze held Mak's. Yes, the king knew the story. All the island knew about the tragedy that had become front-page news. It had been repeated when the king bought Akim, and again during the following years when Akim had won the cup.

"Who would have thought that lovely lady I met at the party was a fine jockey?" He chuckled and let go of Mak's hand.

Mak turned his lips into a polite smile. He didn't need to respond to that rhetorical question. But he knew the answer. Jane's fiancé knew.

As Akim was being led away, Mak walked over. "Just a moment, please." He stared at Akim while examining his own mind and heart. The horse had his eyes on Mak, who laid his hand on Akim's warm, moist neck and whispered, "I forgive you."

Mak was kneeling at the front of the church the following morning when he felt a hand on his shoulder. Looking back, he saw Rev. Russell. Mak stood.

"For a long time," Mak said, "coming in here and getting things right between me and God has been in the back of my mind, and even more so since Jane has spoken her mind to me — more than once."

The reverend's face relaxed into a knowing expression, but he made no comment, apparently sensing that Mak had to make his peace.

"I've been coming to the conclusion that I needed to forgive God for letting Maylea and my baby die." He shook his head. "I don't think that anymore. I think I needed to ask God to forgive me."

"He understands, Mak. God still loves you, and He's still as close as you let Him be."

Mak nodded. "I know that. But it's easier

to accept when things are going well."

"Is it?" the reverend said. "Or do we tend to take God for granted when things are going well?"

Mak stood and looked at the wooden cross on the wall behind the pulpit. The reverend had a point. He'd taken a lot of his blessings for granted. "In the past three years, I've talked about, thought about, questioned, and tried to reason things about life that didn't suit me more than in the rest of my life combined."

"It's a maturing process, Mak."

A defining moment, Mak thought.

"Do you remember the verse I quoted to you before the race?"

"I can't quote it," Mak said, shifting his weight from one foot to the other. "Something about winning the race."

"That was about winning the physical race, Mak. Here, look at the ending of that sentence." He turned the pages of his Bible and read: " 'I press toward the mark for the prize. . . .' " He paused, then read the rest. " 'The prize of the high calling of God in Christ Jesus.' " He closed the Bible. "We have our human races, Mak. But the one that makes the biggest difference is the one we race daily. The spiritual one."

■ ■ ■ ■

"Well Jane," Matilda scolded a few days after the race. "You had enough courage to ride the most powerful horse on the island, and you can't face the likes of Mak Mac-Cauley? Is this my niece talking?"

Jane tried to explain it to herself. Finally, it hit her. "It's like I told you before. Austin would never hurt me. But Mak can."

"Then maybe you should book the next ship back to Texas."

Jane stared into Matilda's challenging eyes. Then she promptly went into her bedroom, changed into her riding clothes, marched out the door, and rode Anise to the ranch.

Big Brown stood in the corral. Mak was brushing Panai. Across from Panai in a niche she hadn't noticed before was the Big Island Cup. Mak had what he wanted. His revenge, his big win. He wasn't talking to Panai, and his face did not have the look of someone who had lost his grief and misery.

Panai gave a low whinny. Jane walked over to the horse and rubbed his face. The horse wasn't angry with her. She heard Mak's quick intake of breath when he saw her.

"How is Chico?"

Mak looked behind her as if expecting someone else. He again focused on the horse. "It's not appendicitis." If he wasn't careful, he might brush a hole in that horse.

"Chico's wife remembered that his dad had a bad reaction to taking salicin. Chico had been taking it for a while for a headache he had after pulling a muscle in his neck."

He laid the brush aside, and she stepped back so he could swing the door open and come out. Again he looked toward the doorway. "The last I heard, they were planning to test further, but they suspect he has an ulcerated stomach from the salicin." He added, with relief in his voice, "That is treatable."

She gestured at the cup. "I see you've given the cup to the one who deserves it — Panai."

"You deserve it, too." He began walking toward the doorway, and she followed.

"I'm not sorry. Chico said I might not win, but I could ride him." While Mak washed his hands at the water pump, she felt her words coming out like a tumbleweed. "He was right. I couldn't win. But Panai could. He did the work. I was just along for the ride. It was the ride of my life, and I won't apologize for it. I just wish you hadn't been so angry about it." She gave him a hard look. "After all, I didn't throw up on him."

He shook the water from his hands and wiped them on the sides of his shirt. She thought he grinned. "Why do you think I was angry?"

She took a deep breath. But it didn't stop the tumbleweed. "Because you didn't really want Panai to win. You wouldn't have anything to hold onto without your grief and misery."

"Jane," he said. "That might be true if you hadn't come into my life. You've changed me. I didn't know just how much until you determined to get on that horse. I knew then you were more important to me than the horse, than the race."

Jane knew that was saying a lot. But did he mean the value of a human being in general . . . or . . . ?

"During the race, I didn't care if Panai came in last or didn't come in at all." He reached out and took hold of her hands. "I wanted you to be safe. For your sake and . . . I did not want Austin to feel the pain of losing someone he loves. Since I'm being honest, I kept thinking that you made me realize that I could love again. God might bring into my life a lovely young woman whom I could come to love, yet . . . I worried that she might not be available —"

His words stopped, and he focused on her left hand, the ring finger. His glance moved to her face and back again, questioning.

"Austin felt that my riding that horse was my racing away from him. He didn't return the ring."

Mak looked pained. "I'm sorry if I caused that. Ruined that for you."

"You are . . . sorry?"

"Yes. No. I mean —"

"Mak, I couldn't accept that ring again. Austin and I both realized we're the best friends in the world. We love each other. But we're not in love. My being your friend has saved me from the prospect of a friendly, boring, good life."

"No. You would make each day exciting just by being in it."

"Well, as I said, I feel like you saved my life."

He stepped closer, and his hand came around her waist. "There's a Chinese saying —"

"Finally," she interrupted. "Why do you think I kept repeating that you saved my life? But go ahead and finish the proverb."

A loving look came into his eyes. "There's a Chinese saying that if you save someone's life, you're responsible for them for the rest of your life."

"Do you mean . . . ?"

"I mean I love you, Jane. I would like nothing better than for you to become my wife. Is there a chance?"

"There is. And I want you to know this, Mak. I want to plan a marriage with you every day of my life. That's where I want to focus. I want to be a wife you can respect and cherish and love."

He put his fingers against her lips. "Let me ask you this. Can you ever forget Austin?"

"No." Her heart began to hammer, anticipating what he was about to say.

"I can't forget Maylea, either. And you're the one who has made me realize I don't have to. But the amazing thing about these hearts of ours is there's room for more love than we can ever realize. I love you completely. You, as you are. There's no competing. I may think of her at times, like when Leia graduates from a class, is baptized. And when she marries, I may think that her mother is watching. But here, you are her mother."

"I know," Jane said. "And I will probably always remember Austin's wealth and think he could probably buy the entire island of Hawaii, and I'll remember his sweet kisses."

"Aarrgh," Mak growled.

"But yours," she teased, "if we ever get that far, could probably make me forget everything else in the world."

"I can live with that," he said. "There's something I've wanted to do for a long time, without feeling guilty . . . or miserable."

He brought his hand up from her waist and gently touched her lips. Hers parted to take in a breath. "Don't say any more," she said. "Show me."

So he did.

His lips were only a breath away. She closed her eyes to experience her own personal, passionate adventure in paradise.

CHAPTER 36

Jane insisted she wanted a simple ceremony, but as plans evolved, Mak began to understand the meaning of everything in Texas being big. These people didn't know the meaning of simple.

"I'm not going to recognize this house when you women get through," Mak grumbled to Matilda and his mom, who were changing everything around.

"You're not supposed to," his mom said.

"Jane can rearrange, or we can build a new house after we're married."

"But that takes time." Matilda's hand shooed him away. "This is a woman thing, trust me," and they insisted upon giving new master bedroom furniture to him and Jane instead of using what had been his mother's.

He didn't even know how to argue with those women.

After receiving a wedding invitation, the

king sent his regrets but offered a guest cottage on the palace grounds for their honeymoon. Since it was such a long boat trip to Oahu, his mother, Matilda, and Leia were taking the king up on the offer instead. Mak and Jane agreed they'd rather stay at his — their — house.

When they'd all had dinner at Russ's house one evening, Jane told Mak they'd have a lifetime for making adventurous trips. And he didn't need a wedding rehearsal; he should just do as he was told.

"You have my condolences," Austin said. He'd also said he wanted to make sure Jane was happily married before he left the island. Mak had gone with him to look over some property Austin might buy, and Mak thought that had a lot to do with Austin prolonging his stay. Austin told him he planned to go back and marry Rebecca. He'd already sent a letter so Rebecca could be making her plans.

The day finally arrived.

Doing as he was told, Mak holed up in Austin's hotel room. He did not see Jane all day and was told he wasn't supposed to.

When evening came, Austin drove him to the beach.

The public was invited, and it looked to Mak like more people lined the three-mile stretch of beach than at Christmastime. But then, Jane was now more of a celebrity than Santa. She'd become an island hero, and all the little girls wanted to be jockeys. Jane said they'd probably settle for being equestriennes.

Austin drove Mak right up to where chairs had been set out for personally invited guests. Mr. Buckley stood with his hands folded in front of his black formal suit and top hat.

Mak walked down the aisle, looking from side to side, greeting the guests.

But where was Jane?

Reverend Russell stood smiling, in a light green robe beneath a white arbor elaborately decorated with every color and type of flower imaginable. "Stand here," the reverend told him, and Mak stood at one side of the arbor and faced his guests.

Music began. Mak looked to the side where a band of men he knew, some of his own paniolos, strummed love songs on their bragas. One began to sing. Pilar and Susanne, in light green dresses, passed out leis like the ones the two girls were wearing to the guests in chairs.

But where was Jane?

Seeing a movement up the beach, he thought his heart might beat right out of his chest. Riding up on her little white pony was his little girl. Mr. Buckley aided her in dismounting and handed her a basket.

In a white dress with a green sash and wearing a colorful lei, she paraded down the aisle, carefully dropping orchid petals. Seeing that she had some remaining when she reached the arbor, she looked concerned, then turned the basket up and let the rest of the petals float to where Jane should be standing. With a big smile, she turned, sat in a chair beside his mom, and smoothed her skirt, looking like a little lady.

Hearing a cry go up and applause begin, he looked. Big Brown was galloping along the beach with Jane astride him, a long white cover over her lap and thighs and streaming out behind her like a wave on an ocean.

Several persons helped her get rid of the cover, groomed her long, brown, sun-brushed hair that took on the golden glow of the sun. While love songs were being sung, Jane's father escorted her down the aisle.

Happiness flooded Mak's soul, yes, his soul as well as his heart, as he thanked God for this gift that, not long ago, he could never have imagined could be his. White flowers and green leaves encircled Jane's head. She carried a bouquet of white orchids and green leaves, with long green ribbons flowing from it.

As the color of the sky changed to deep gold with a touch of crimson, Pilar and Susanne handed both the bride and groom a white and green lei.

"You may exchange the leis as a symbol of your love for each other," the reverend said, and Mak slipped the lei over Jane's head and lifted her long, soft, fragrant hair, taking a moment to revel in the feel of it as he had never dared do before.

She placed her lei over his head.

Mak could not take his eyes from her. The reverend said many things, and one that registered was, "What God has joined together, let no man put asunder."

At the appropriate time, Mak slipped on her vacant finger a band set with small emeralds that matched the larger set of the engagement ring they'd picked out together.

She said it had to be green, in memory of the night of the sunset when he'd taken her breath away.

"I now pronounce you man and wife. You may kiss the bride."

And he did.

After a moment, Jane leaned away. "Remember your instructions to a racehorse.

Don't give it your all until you come into the home stretch."

He exhaled heavily. "Good advice."

The reverend had the guests stand and led them in singing "Blest Be the Tie That Binds."

Mak and Jane hurried up the aisle. He mounted Big Brown and lifted Jane in front of him. As they rode across the beach in the golden, crimson evening toward the ranch, Jane turned her face toward him. "I've practiced this," she said. "Aloha au la oe."

Thanking God for his being the most blessed man in the world, Mak said, "I love you, too."